GOOD BEHAVIOR

BOOK 5 OF THE *JOHNSON* FAMILY SERIES

DELANEY DIAMOND

Good Behavior

Copyright © 2016, Delaney Diamond

Garden Avenue Press
Atlanta, Georgia

ISBN: 978-1-940636-41-2

Dear Reader,

This is it. The last novel in the Johnson Family saga. It's bittersweet because I've grown attached to the Johnsons as I've watched them over the past couple of years—falling in love, breaking hearts, and expanding their family.

This book contains all the elements you've come to love and expect. The family's wealth and power is still on display. So is the sense of family, their love for each other, and the manner in which they fiercely protect anyone they love.

I dedicate this one to you, for so fully embracing this saga. Thank you from the bottom of my heart.

Get ready for another sweet, sensual, passionate romance—Delaney Diamond style! And without further ado, I introduce you to the next couple who will fall in love and have their happily ever after: Diana Cambridge and Xavier Johnson.

.

PROLOGUE

Two months ago

Before Xavier Johnson met Sasha Fulsom for dinner, he sensed there would be bad news. On the telephone, her voice didn't hold its usual anticipatory breathlessness, and he suspected their relationship was coming to an end.

Now it was official. He and Sasha were over.

He scribbled his name on the credit card receipt and handed it back to the server, who in turn thanked him profusely for the generous tip and left them alone again.

Across the table, Sasha checked her makeup in a small compact. As usual, her hair and face were immaculate. She turned heads wherever she went, and had turned his the first time he saw her at an event in Los Angeles. Two phone calls, one bouquet of flowers, and an extravagant dinner later, they'd become lovers.

"Are you ready to go?" Xavier asked.

She nodded, the candlelight flickering off her ebony skin.

They exited the Oasis Room of Agua, a high-end Latin fusion restaurant she'd chosen a few miles outside the city—a venue they'd visited before, not only for the excellent cuisine, but because the owners offered unparalleled confidentiality with various private rooms. They walked down a hallway to the separate entrance reserved for high profile diners, silent and each immersed in their own thoughts. The cobblestone walkway led through a courtyard to a concealed parking lot where valets waited.

"So this is it." Sasha kept her eyes averted. "You can still talk me out of it."

Xavier couldn't see her face very well because the short bob covered most of her features as she looked out at the parking lot. "If I can talk you out of it, you're not ready to get married."

"I'm ready for marriage, but the man I want to marry doesn't want me."

He didn't reply. If he denied the accuracy of the statement, he'd be a liar.

She shrugged her slight shoulders. "I knew it wouldn't last when we got involved."

Xavier lifted an eyebrow. "Oh really?"

"You're looking for a specific type of woman."

"You have me all figured out," he said, mildly amused.

"A little." She tilted her head in an assessing way. "Your ideal woman must be uncomplicated, unpretentious, and down-to-earth. None of which I am. Oh, and she must have maternal instincts." She extended her hand so the light picked up the diamonds on her wrist. "I'm complicated and certainly not down-to-earth. I enjoy the finer things in life. I'm very demanding, although you managed to keep me at a distance, and there's not a maternal bone in my body. We were never going to be more than just lovers."

She said the words with certainty, prompting Xavier to ask, "Then why did you continue seeing me?"

Sasha twisted the engagement ring on her finger—one that had been placed there within the past two weeks, to Xavier's surprise, by a man Xavier knew very little about except that he was twenty years her senior, rich, and indulged her every whim.

Her brow wrinkled before her gaze met his again. "Because the sex is amazing," she quipped.

Xavier let out a loud laugh. "I guess I should be flattered."

A coy smile flitted across her lips. "The truth is, I thought I could change you. Classic female denial. I realized you wouldn't change when you never introduced me to your family."

She spoke lightly, playfully, but he sensed the hurt beneath the words, and guilt twisted in his chest. Not a single member of his family knew he was seeing her. Sasha was attractive, cultured, and comfortable in their world. Exactly the kind of woman he should choose for a life partner. Add in their compatibility in bed, and she was almost perfect.

Except she didn't want children, and for Xavier, that was a deal breaker.

His siblings were all moving forward with domesticated life, and he envied them. Gavin's wife was pregnant with their third child. Trent was getting married. Ivy and Lucas were engaged, and Cyrus's reconciliation with his wife Daniella had resulted in a son and another baby on the way.

Seeing them so content made him long even more for the same, and the only kind of woman who would be right for him was one who shared his views on family.

Sasha spread her fingers and stared at the brilliant rock. "When are you going to settle down?"

"Eventually."

"You're almost thirty-six years old. Your youngest brother is beating you to the altar."

"I'm still young. I'll settle down when the time is right."

She punched a text into her phone and then dropped the device back into her purse. "I'm a little jealous of this future woman. Silly, isn't it?"

"We wouldn't have worked. You said so yourself."

She didn't respond, only intertwining her fingers in front of her.

Seconds later, a black SUV pulled up. The driver jumped out, came around to their side, and opened the door.

Neither of them moved. This was it. The end of their affair. This was the end of a third relationship since he'd returned home less than two years ago, which meant women cycled in and out of his life an average of every six months—a cringe-worthy statistic that did not bode well for any long-term relationship.

Sasha ran a hand down his chest. Her fingers folded around his tie, and she gently tugged, pulling him down for a kiss. He allowed it, because he understood this was good-bye.

Their lips connected and his body stirred to life. One arm snaked around her waist, and he pulled her hard against him, kissing her with more passion.

She melted against him and moaned. The familiar sound lit his blood on fire, hardening his body. Those mewling noises were simply a prelude to the more boisterous sounds of lovemaking she made when he thrust into her so hard and deep she screamed his name and begged for mercy.

Sasha inhaled sharply and pulled back, eyes wild and filled with desire.

"One last time," she whispered, touching a hand to his cheek, her eyes pleading.

No matter how much his body burned for her, Xavier couldn't. "You're wearing another man's ring." He spoke the words softly and without accusation.

Her mouth twisted ruefully in regret. "That I am."

She pressed her lips to his again, briefer this time, then quickly pulled away and turned to the vehicle, but not before he saw the sheen of tears in her eyes.

"Good-bye, Xavier."

Climbing into the SUV, she didn't give him a second glance. In the interior, he couldn't see her face behind the black tint of the windows.

For a long time after they drove away, Xavier stood on the sidewalk with an emptiness in his gut. Her words came in a chanting taunt.

When are you going to settle down?

He wiped a hand across his mouth, lips still tingling from the taste of her.

He'd have to be a little bit more patient, it seemed.

CHAPTER ONE

Present day

Xavier looked up from the document on his desk and rolled his stiff shoulders. Glancing at the Audemars Piguet timepiece on his wrist, he muttered, "Damn."

Later than he thought.

He removed the oval metal-framed glasses and swiveled in the mahogany executive chair. Rubbing a thumb along the bridge of his nose, he looked out at the dusky sky. No matter how many times he told himself he would leave early, he ended up staying late.

A low grumble had him clutching his stomach, which meant after a trip to the copy room, he needed to stop on the way home for a bite to eat. The snack from the break room had only served to tease his appetite.

He gathered the pages and walked toward the copy room. In the quiet hallway, the cleaning woman dusted the awards and pictures covering the walls. Her cinnamon-brown face turned in his direction. "Good night, Mr. Johnson."

"How are you this evening, Linda?"

"Fine, sir."

He paused. "How did Vincent's surgery go?" Her husband had been admitted for a sinus endoscopy a few days ago.

Linda's eyes lit up at the question. "Very good, sir. Thank you for asking. In and out in one day, like the doctors promised. He took the week off and will be back to work next week."

"Excellent." He gave her the thumbs-up sign and continued to his destination down the hall.

The large room contained several copiers, a fax machine, and a computer terminal. Shelves stocked with paper and other office supplies lined the bottom half of one wall, with the top half available for use as a workstation.

Xavier stuffed the pages into the nearest copier feeder and hit *Start*. The sheets ran through easily, but five pages in, the machine stopped and let out three high-pitched warning beeps. Frowning, he removed the sheets that remained to be copied, found a stuck page and removed that, too. But a light continued to blink on the console.

"Come on," he muttered. Just his luck. Right when he was ready to leave, something kept him in the office.

He lifted the lid, searching in vain for the problem. After several minutes of lifting and rattling parts of the machine, he slammed a hand atop the copier in frustration.

What was wrong with this thing?

"Come on!" he growled.

"Need some help?" a quiet voice asked.

Xavier swung around. Diana Cambridge, his brother's efficient and professional executive assistant, stood behind him, an amused sparkle in her large round eyes.

"What are you still doing here?" he asked.

"Going through sales projections." She walked farther into the room, her ample hips swaying as her heels clicked on the tile.

A plus-size sister with short ebony curls, she wore her confidence like a suit of armor. They seldom ran into each other because of the sheer size of the floor, but whenever they did, she captured his attention with her eye-catching ensembles.

Today's outfit consisted of large gold earrings and chunky jewelry paired with a dark green ruffled blouse and black pencil skirt. He couldn't help but notice how the skirt showed off her long legs.

She was easily five feet eight without the black pumps that brought her within inches of the top of his head.

"Don't tell me Trenton has you working late while he's at home."

"Oh no, Trenton would never do that." She laughed easily, her face becoming animated, and a dimple in her left cheek made an appearance. Breathing in her fragrance, he smelled vanilla and coconut. Simple. Natural. Unpretentious.

"Would you like some help?" She cocked a brow, and Xavier realized he'd been staring.

Shaking off the temporary fog, he said, "Yes, I would." He waved at the offending machine. "There's a piece of paper stuck in there somewhere, but I can't find it."

"Let me see what I can do."

He stood back and let her go to work.

"I think I know what the problem is," she murmured, bending over and reaching toward the back of the machine.

Xavier went still, nostrils flaring at the provocative pose. His gaze fixed on how the skirt molded to her ass, hugging enough to give a good impression of the lift and width of her bottom without being indecent. He tugged on his suddenly restrictive tie.

"Got it!"

His gaze shifted up. Victorious, Diana held a torn piece of paper between her fingers. She snapped the lid closed on what looked like a hidden compartment—at least one he hadn't found—and the blinking light disappeared.

"That little thing caused so much trouble?" he asked.

"Afraid so." She tossed the scrap in the trash. "I'll take those."

He handed her the pages.

"How many?" she asked.

"Ten."

While she ran the copies, Xavier alternated between watching her and watching pages fly out of the machine.

When he started at Johnson Enterprises eighteen months ago—his family's beer and restaurant conglomerate—he and Diana spent a few weeks working closely together. She helped him get settled until he hired is own assistant. She had intrigued him right away, not only with her knowledge but her warm personality. Yet he'd kept his distance. She'd been married at the time, and then there was the other sticky issue—the fact that he was the chief operating officer of the company where she worked. Nonetheless, whenever she came near, tension filled his muscles and his senses went on high alert.

Diana stacked the copies together and handed them to him. "Here you go."

"Thank you. You're a lifesaver. Now go home."

"I will," she said with a laugh. "Right after I stop off to get a bite to eat."

He opened his mouth to inquire where she was headed, but stopped. He was friendly, but to a point. He never wanted an employee to feel as if he was infringing on their time and space.

"Enjoy your dinner," he said.

"Can I help you with anything else?" There were a few things she could help him with. None of them work-related.

"I have everything I need." He held up the stack of papers. "Thank you."

"Good night."

****

The Waterfront and Pike Place Market—the oldest continuously operating market in the country—were among Seattle's most visited sites. Diana loved the area but tended to avoid the mazelike market because of the throng of Seattleites and tourists who swarmed the buildings after the early morning hours. They came to see the famous fishmongers with their theatrical yelling and tossing of the daily catch and to purchase fresh produce, flowers, and products from local artisans.

At this hour of night, the market had already closed, and the activity on the waterfront had died down. Diana was craving a burger, and if she'd been smart, she would have bought one from The Brew Pub, the casual dining chain owned by the Johnson family and located on the first floor of their building. But she hadn't been smart, and given the late hour, too distracted by work. That's why she was staring up at the Burger Escape menu, trying to decide between a mushroom burger and an avocado burger.

"We have to stop meeting like this." The words vibrated in the air, his voice was so rich and smooth and attention-grabbing.

Xavier, the second oldest of the Johnson siblings, stood behind her in line, looking as freshly pressed as he did when she helped him in the copy room, in a charcoal three-piece suit, charcoal tie, and white shirt. A familiar prickling sensation crept over her, crawled under her skin, and invaded her bones. He was one fine man, his complexion a rich brown, the same dark hue as a bar of chocolate. While his brothers were all clean-shaven, the short, neat hairs of a circle beard framed his generous lips, leaving the strength of his jaw exposed.

All of the Johnsons had a refined, polished appearance. Anyone who didn't know who they were could tell they came from money, but there was something about *him*. An underlying current of…something. Not quite civilized, not quite untamed, an earthiness magnified by the dreadlocks and facial hair.

"We had the same idea," Diana said.

"So it seems. This is going to sound crazy coming from a man whose family owns a casual dining restaurant, but I've been craving a burger all day." He flashed an engaging smile, friendly and absolutely stunning in its brilliance.

"I'm in the same boat. I wanted something big, gooey, delicious, and utterly bad for me."

Xavier laughed. "Sounds like an excellent idea. I'll join you."

"You will?"

"Don't sound so surprised." Amusement filled his dark eyes.

"I figured you came for the grilled chicken salad."

"Oh sure. That's why everybody comes to Burger Escape."

She covered her mouth and giggled. Xavier always made her laugh. "I have to admit, I assumed you'd be interested in a gourmet place. You know, a restaurant that serves seaweed on a bun or something."

"First of all, that sounds absolutely unappetizing. Second of all, I enjoy gourmet food like anyone else—well, maybe not as much as Cyrus. Don't tell him I said that."

"I won't." She pulled an imaginary zipper across her lips.

"But my vice is junk food. I love a good hotdog, too."

"Really?" She was learning all kinds of interesting tidbits about him.

"Oh yeah." Xavier stepped out of the way so a man carrying a tray filled with burgers, fries, and drinks could pass. "A good Chicago dog or chili cheese dog brings me this close to nirvana every time." He held up his finger and thumb a small distance apart.

"I happen to love a good dog myself. There's a food truck I stalk that's always downtown called—"

"Dog World," they said at the same time.

She blinked. "Yes."

"No seaweed anywhere near that menu."

"True. And they pile on the chili and cheese, don't they?"

"You can barely see the hot dog."

"I know! It's terrible, but so good." She giggled again.

She saw warmth in his eyes, but a razor-sharp shrewdness, as well.

"Since we're on the same page, why don't we have dinner together? My treat."

A smidge of heat invaded her stomach. Dinner with Xavier Johnson sounded almost too intimate. "No. I'm fine. I'm going to grab my meal, and then call a car to take me home."

"No way. I'd be happy to take you home after dinner."

"I couldn't ask you—"

"I insist. Besides, you saved me from the big, mean copier that was eating my pages. Consider my offer to be a debt repaid. If you don't mind, of course."

Of course she didn't. Their interaction felt easy and fluid. She wanted to spend time with him and had privately acknowledged her attraction to him even before her divorce was final last year. To her shame, he'd infiltrated her fantasies on more than one occasion, performing all manner of carnal acts her husband would never engage in.

Diana shook off the hesitation. "All right, Mr. Johnson, I'll allow you to repay your very huge debt by buying me dinner."

This time, it was he who laughed.

CHAPTER TWO

They took the meals to go, but before exiting the restaurant, Xavier removed his jacket. "Here you go. It's chilly out there."

"No, I'm fine." Alarm filled Diana's eyes, as if she couldn't imagine taking his clothing.

He cocked a brow. "*I'm* fine, in these long sleeves." He held up one arm. "You're going to need this."

She reluctantly took the jacket. "Thank you," she said. The sleeves came all the way down to her knuckles. After she rolled them up, they took their food and exited the restaurant.

After a leisurely stroll along the pier, Xavier led them to an empty metal bench, where he placed his soda, fries, a burger smothered in chili, and one topped with guacamole and bacon on the seat between them. He unpacked the chili burger and sank his teeth into the bread and meat, keeping his legs spread to avoid dripping chili onto his pants. He bounced his head up and down in satisfaction.

"Delicious," he said around the mouthful of food.

Diana's burger was topped with mushrooms and melted cheese. She took a bite and nodded in satisfaction. "Excellent."

They ate in silence for a few minutes, but he caught her glancing at him out of the corner of her eye.

"Why do you keep looking at me?" Xavier asked.

She gave an embarrassed laugh. "I'm stumped. You're the COO of Johnson Enterprises and you're eating hamburgers on the waterfront. I don't know, it seems weird."

"Not so weird. My family owns The Brew Pub. We don't exactly serve fine cuisine there. Besides, how could you not like this? Hell, I've been to places where these hamburgers could be the best meal someone had for the week."

"Overseas in Africa?"

Xavier shook his head. "Here, actually. Approximately fifteen percent of Americans live below the poverty level. That's about forty-five million people."

Her eyes widened. "That's a lot."

"In the greatest country in the world," Xavier said, not bothering to hide the sarcasm.

They ate in silence for a bit. When Diana had eaten half her burger, she started on the fries.

"So, I know about your time in Africa," she spoke slowly, tentatively, as if concerned about prying. "Which countries did you visit?"

Xavier swallowed a morsel of the burger. "I spent most of my time in the western part of the continent—Senegal, Ghana, Liberia, Côte d'Ivoire. I spent some time in Asia and South America, too. In South America, we worked on a project to protect the Amazon and keep the indigenous people undisturbed."

"I didn't know that."

He nodded. He refrained from telling her how the effects of deforestation were far-reaching, creating an imbalance in nature and threatening the climate. Not only in South America, but around the world. Government officials all looked the other way and encouraged the "development," concerned only about short-term gains instead of looking at the long term desecration of land and people. The whole situation disgusted him.

Diana sipped soda through a straw. "What did you work on in Africa?"

Xavier crushed the wax paper in his fist, dropped it onto the bench, and picked up the second hamburger. "Much of the same.

Making sure local communities weren't taken advantage of by outside corporations. My family traced our ancestry to Senegal, and that's where I spent a lot of my time. When I arrived there, it felt almost like...going home."

Her expression softened. "Do you miss it?"

"Sometimes. I'm glad to be home with my family, but the changes I'd hoped to make there didn't come to fruition." His jaw hardened in disgust at the memory of how he'd lost his temper, the angry mob, and his incarceration. Senegal was without a doubt his biggest disappointment in life.

Altogether, he'd dedicated almost fifteen years to working around the world. From the time he turned eighteen, he spent most of his breaks in other countries, and after college, volunteerism became more or less a full-time profession. His mother had been his biggest champion, encouraging him to pursue his passion, even though it meant butting heads with his father's desire for him to work at the company.

"So, what does Diana Cambridge do when she leaves the office?"

She did this thing where she wrinkled her nose. It was something he'd never noticed before. Cute.

"Not much. Diana goes home and spends time with her son."

"Your son's name is Andre, right? How old is he now?"

Her eyebrows lifted in surprise, as if she couldn't believe he knew her son's name, but he made a habit of memorizing details about staff, even the ones he rarely interacted with.

She licked a drop of ketchup off her thumb, and Xavier froze, temporarily losing his train of thought. The quick movement incited a riot of sensation in his pants.

"Andre is seven and wrapping up second grade with all A's and B's. He drives me crazy sometimes, but I can't imagine my life without him. He's bright and funny and has a generous spirit. Aside from the fact that he never picks up after himself, I couldn't ask for a better kid."

The bright-eyed little boy had inherited her big doe eyes. In one of the pictures on her desk, the boy looked about six years old, showing off missing front teeth to the camera. In the other, his face was a bit more solemn, and he was dressed in a school uniform and toting a backpack. Still another showed the two of them cheesing for the camera, dressed as a witch and a goblin for Halloween.

"You mentioned something about a cousin once?" he inquired.

"Mhmm. My cousin, Camille, lives with me. We're originally from the Bay area, but I moved here first when I got married. I'm, um…divorced now."

"How long were you married?"

She shifted, and he wondered if he'd gotten too personal.

"Eight years. Andre didn't understand why we weren't living together as a family anymore and misses his father, but my ex-husband sees him every other weekend, and when Rodrick—my ex—isn't too busy during the week, he picks him up from school and they go to dinner and have male bonding time."

"Sounds like you have a great relationship with your ex-husband."

She smiled tightly.

Huh. Maybe not.

Diana glanced at her watch, a Cartier timepiece Trenton had given her to celebrate her three-year anniversary with the firm. "I better get going soon."

"Of course." Xavier didn't know if she really needed to leave or if she simply wanted to avoid the conversation about her personal life, but he wolfed down the rest of the burger and they both tossed their containers into the trash.

He stuffed his hands into his pockets as they walked slowly back to his SUV. He'd enjoyed the food and company and was reluctant for the evening to end. Strange how a simple evening out with someone he barely knew could bring such satisfaction.

After he'd started the car, he turned to look at her in the passenger seat. "Thank you for joining me for dinner."

"Thank *you* for paying. The meal was just what I'd been hoping for. Something completely bad for me. Tomorrow I'll go back to eating nuts and berries." She laughed sarcastically, smoothing her hands over her ample thighs.

The movement caught Xavier's eye, and his fingers tightened on the leather wheel. He wondered if her legs were as soft as they looked.

Shifting his attention to the rearview mirror, he said, "I don't think you need to worry about that."

"I need to be good and stop being so bad." She crossed one smooth thigh over the other and his eyes dipped once again to the expanse of exposed brown skin.

"Nothing wrong with doing things that are bad for you every now and again. Keeps life interesting." He cleared his throat and eased backward, but hit the brakes when a pedestrian crossed in his path.

"Are you saying you do bad things?" Her voice was softer, teasing.

In the darkness of the vehicle, her large doe eyes stared back at him. The question was suggestive at best, inappropriate at worse. What was she really asking him?

His eyes zeroed in on the pulse beating at the base of her throat, and his own pulse thudded a little faster. "I always try to be on my best behavior."

Always. All his life. He only slept with one woman at a time, and he wasn't a cynical shark like the eldest, Cyrus—who'd been groomed to be more like their father than any of them.

"I don't always succeed," he finished quietly.

Diana licked her lips, and tension mounted in the interior of the vehicle. "I can understand that," she said, swallowing. "It's a lot harder than people think. Being good, I mean."

He kept his gaze on her. "Definitely. Especially when temptation is staring you right in the face. It can be hard as hell."

There was a minute reaction—a spark in the depths of her eyes, before she retreated with a vigorous nod and focused on her hands. "Very," she muttered, letting out a quiet breath that sounded shaky.

Xavier gripped the steering wheel at that soft, feminine sound and fought the sudden urge to drag her across the console and kiss her hard and thoroughly. This was why he'd kept his distance all these months, and he should have never spent this time alone with her. He didn't only find Diana intriguing; he was undeniably attracted to her. That attraction threatened everything he knew about himself.

"The good one" was what friends, family, and the media had called Xavier for years. The one who'd forsaken his family's wealth to fight injustice around the world. The one who—except for an angry confrontation in Senegal years ago, which landed him in jail with plenty of regret and time to reflect—had always exemplified good behavior.

Spending time with Diana made him want to forget his good behavior. And show her just how bad he could be.

CHAPTER THREE

Diana's two-story home was located in a quiet suburb. The house sat in the middle of a row of similar houses on a tree-lined street. She and Xavier walked slowly up to the front door, and all she could think about was how sad it was that this evening was the most fun she'd had in a long time.

At Burger Escape, she had texted Camille to let her know she'd be running a little behind, but Camille didn't mind. Their arrangement worked out perfectly for both of them. Diana paid all the bills and in exchange, Camille had use of Diana's car as she looked for work, got Andre off the bus each day, and watched him until Diana came home.

Standing under the light at the front door, she gazed up at Xavier. "Thank you again for dinner."

His smile exposed perfect, eggshell-white teeth. "I'm glad you had a good time."

Despite the geniality in his face, his eyes held a watchfulness that put Diana on edge. She shifted from one foot to the other, hesitant to say good night but knowing she needed to. She couldn't remember the last time she'd enjoyed a man's company so much.

"I'm going to need that." Xavier inclined his head at the jacket she still wore.

"Oh!" Her cheeks flushed hot. No wonder he was still standing there. "I completely forgot." She hurriedly removed the article of clothing, losing not only its warmth but the comforting fragrance of his cologne and his natural earthy aroma embedded in the fabric.

He took his time putting it on, pushing his long arms through the sleeves and taking his time rolling them down.

Finally, their eyes met. "Have a good night," he said.

"I will. You, too."

Diana went into the house, but took a quick second to lean against the door and regroup. She pressed a hand over her rapidly beating heart and inhaled deeply. Easing over to the window, she peeked through the curtains and watched as Xavier swung his body up into the SUV.

Goodness, that man is magnificent.

The light in the living room flicked on, and she jumped back from the window.

Camille stood at the foot of the stairs with both hands on her full hips in a pink robe and a satin scarf bulging with rollers.

"Why did you do that?" Diana demanded in a harsh whisper.

"What are you doing?" her cousin sang.

"Nothing," Diana said defensively. She removed her shoes and let them dangle from two fingers on her right hand.

"When you texted you were eating a late dinner with a co-worker, you didn't mention he looked like that. Is he Bryant?" her cousin asked.

Bryant worked at the firm and made no secret of his interest in Diana. Her co-worker Jaclyn thought he was a good catch.

"No."

"Who is he then? He is *fine*." Her cousin's eyes sparkled with interest. At twenty-five, Camille was a full nine years younger than Diana and shorter, but with the same full-figured curves.

"Xavier Johnson, the chief operating officer of Johnson Enterprises." She let the words sink in.

Camille's eyes grew wide as coasters. "Well, aren't you special? That's quite a step up."

"He gave me a ride home. That's all," Diana said. She downplayed the lift, but did feel special.

"Today it's a ride. Tomorrow it's some tongue." Camille wiggled her eyebrows.

"Would you stop!" Diana walked over and thumped her cousin's arm.

Camille giggled. "Why? Dinner with one of your bosses sounds like a way to dive back into the dating game, and you know you need to."

"I'm already thinking about it. Bryant, remember?"

"Bryant is a mere employee," Camille said airily. "Why have hamburger when you can eat filet mignon?"

Diana rolled her eyes. "That man is not thinking about me, believe me." Although the thought of him noticing her did spread a warm sensation all along the insides of her chest.

"Maybe not, but *you're* thinking about him."

"I admit he's...good-looking," Diana conceded.

"Good-looking *as hell*. So tall and solid-looking." Camille did a little wiggle.

"*But*, I'm realistic. I don't live in fantasyland like some people." Diana looked pointedly at her cousin. "Besides, I told you already, I'm not sure I'm ready to start dating again."

"It's been a year. You can't continue to let your douchebag ex have so much control over your life."

"Camille, he's Andre's father."

"So what?" She propped a fist on her hip and pouted.

"He lets me stay in this house when he could be making money off of it."

"Because for years, you turned over almost every dime you made to help him invest in his real estate business. Cambridge Real Estate should be half yours. He owes you. Letting you stay here is the least he could do, especially after making you suffer through years of no sex. Bastard."

When she'd gotten involved with Rodrick, she'd thought it was sweet that he wanted to wait until marriage to have sex—old-fashioned, but sweet. On their honeymoon she learned the truth. He didn't like sex. Intercourse turned him off. They'd been married for eight years, and lived the latter seven in complete celibacy. Seven. Long. Years.

"That's enough. We both know Rod won't win husband of the year, but staying here allows me to save up money to eventually get a place of my own."

"I'm glad you finally left him. That was no way to live."

Camille was right. She should have left Rodrick years ago but had tried to make her marriage work. Her parents were still married, even after her father's infidelity and two years of financial stress after her mother was laid off.

She'd wanted a marriage that could weather the bad times, too. Despite her efforts, the situation with her ex only became worse. Because they weren't having sex, he believed she was cheating on him and during the last few years of their marriage, he constantly accused her of being unfaithful.

Diana yawned.

"Tired?" her cousin asked.

"Yep. Long day. How's Dre?"

"Fast asleep. He got his homework done. Why do they give seven-year-olds so much homework? He took a shower like a good boy and then went straight to bed."

"I thought I'd get home in time to tuck him in, but I guess I'm too late."

Camille waved a dismissive hand. "He's fine. I tucked him in for you."

"I appreciate you." Diana blew Camille a kiss. "I'm going up to check on him."

"I'm going to the kitchen for a late night snack."

"Stop eating all my ice cream," Diana grumbled, climbing the stairs.

"Stop buying it and I won't," Camille shot back. The drag of her slippers along the hardwood floor stopped. "By the way, I left you some reading material on your bedside table."

Diana rolled her eyes. "Camille." Every few months, an unsolicited book showed up offering advice about better orgasms, how to please a man, or daring sex positions.

"Check it out. You might learn something. Oh, if you need time to practice on one of your men, let me know. Stay out late, spend the night, whatever. You know I'll watch Dre."

Diana sent a grateful smile over the wooden railing to her cousin below. "Thanks, but I don't have a man yet."

"It's only a matter of time before you do. You've got to stop being such a goody two-shoes. Remember, well-behaved women seldom get what they want," Camille sang, strutting away.

Diana shook her head and laughed to herself. She climbed the rest of the stairs and walked to the middle bedroom where her son slept. Cracking the door, she peeped in on Andre. The night light cast an ambient halo in the dark room, and he was fast asleep in the middle of the twin bed, arms spread wide and the bed linens twisted around his legs.

Resting her temple to the doorjamb, Diana stared at her baby. She'd been hesitant to have a child in the midst of her problems with Rodrick, but he'd been insistent. Now she couldn't imagine her life without her little man. He'd made the years of loneliness and rejection from his father tolerable.

Diana quietly closed the door and went to the master bedroom. Inside, a king-sized bed dominated the floor space in a room decorated in neutral tones—brown, tan, and olive. She undressed and climbed into bed, glancing at the book lying on the table: *10 O-inducing Positions for Plus-Size Women.* Sighing, she dropped the book in the drawer with the others she hadn't read, and slammed the drawer shut.

Lying on her side, she considered the evening with Xavier. Was there someone in his life? He was rich, powerful, and very sexy. A man like him couldn't possibly be without regular female companionship.

She sniffed her arm. The faint scent of him lingered in her skin from the jacket, sending tingles down her spine—a longing for more contact. Not from a piece of cloth, but from warm flesh. Hard, male, chocolate flesh.

Diana moaned, restlessly turning and throwing a leg over her body pillow, the only company she ever had in this bed. She'd gone without sex for too long—seven years plus the past year since her divorce equaled eight years of celibacy. That's why she couldn't get Xavier out of her mind. That's why she couldn't stop thinking about what he'd be like in bed. No doubt he'd be masterful. Controlling.

Sex with him would not only be enjoyable, she was certain it could be damn near life-changing.

CHAPTER FOUR

He'd known something was wrong, and now his suspicions were confirmed.

Quietly tapping his fingers on the wooden surface of the oval meeting table in his office, Xavier scanned the preliminary notes the auditors had sent. His brothers Trenton and Gavin waited for his feedback, the silence only disrupted by the soothing trickle of a tabletop fountain in the corner, cycling water from tilted stone pitchers into a bowl filled with stones.

Like other major beer manufacturers, Johnson Brewing Company expanded through the procurement of smaller craft breweries in an effort to increase production, expand their offerings, and seize greater market share. For some time they'd been in talks to purchase Morse Brewing, a family-owned establishment in Missouri. The deal would be their largest purchase to date, and perhaps their most advantageous acquisition thus far.

Nathan Morse owned and managed the company with his two younger brothers. Even his wife—his high school sweetheart—worked at the company. The brothers started brewing beer in their garage and expanded into a multimillion dollar operation based on great-tasting beer and excellent customer service. Morse Brewing offered a large skilled staff and a second midwestern location that served to expand JBC's presence in a part of the country that would improve distribution to vendors and the family restaurants. The

Morse Brewing brand—from the sense of family to the focus on producing great products and providing excellent customer service—perfectly matched Johnson Brewing Company's brand and vision.

Yet as they'd neared the close of the deal, Xavier had developed reservations. Disquiet nagged at him, and now the auditors had mentioned a red flag.

"What's wrong?" Gavin asked to his right.

Gavin had recently completed a brewmaster certification, a fitting complement to his chemistry background. He'd taken over quality control of the breweries, but was also the face of Johnson Brewing Company, playing up his action-adventure past. Their Super Bowl commercial, which used green screen special effects to show him parachuting out of an airplane, rock climbing without gear, and swimming with sharks, had been a hit and trended online.

He'd had his thrills over the years, engaging in dangerous and physically demanding stunts around the world, but was settled down now that he was married. He stuck to less dangerous pursuits, like chasing his two toddlers around his estate.

"According to the auditors, all of the accounts receivables samples they chose came back one hundred percent accurate. Not a single discrepancy," Xavier said.

"Meaning?" Gavin said.

"That's almost impossible. There are always discrepancies, even if they're minor." No one kept such perfect books. Xavier rubbed his forehead. He'd have to alert Cyrus, the CEO, currently in the UK ironing out details for a possible expansion of their facilities over there. "How are we coming on those sales figures?" he asked Trenton, who sat to his left.

While Gavin and Xavier's complexions were dark brown, Trenton—who was actually a cousin, but whom they referred to as a brother because he had grown up with them—had fair skin and green eyes.

"Diana's putting the numbers together for the new sales projections, and I should have those soon," his brother answered.

At the mention of Diana's name, Xavier's shoulders tensed. He almost smelled the delicate scent of vanilla and coconut that had remained in his jacket after their meal on the pier.

He placed the pages on the table. "How soon can you have those numbers for me?" he asked.

"By next week. When Diana's finished, I'll review them and make sure the figures are correct before I hand them over to you."

He didn't expect anything less. Trenton's relaxed, gregarious personality concealed a dogged dedication to detail.

"I'm surprised you can even think about work, with your wedding coming so soon." Gavin's light brown eyes, which matched their late father's, held a teasing light.

"I'm hanging in there," Trenton said.

Xavier scrubbed a hand across his jaw. "Listen, it's the end of the day, so let's wrap up this meeting. I need more time to think, and I have plans later."

"You have plans?" Trenton raised an eyebrow.

"Yes," Xavier muttered, wishing he hadn't said a word. Being in a close-knit family meant they constantly pried into his personal life, and there was nothing exciting or interesting about meeting his personal business manager to review his investments and charitable donations.

"Care to share who you're having dinner with?" Gavin asked. He and Trenton looked at each other across the table, each wearing a smirk on his face.

"Wait, let me answer that," Trenton volunteered. "Mind your own business, am I right?"

"You know me so well, little brother," Xavier replied.

Gavin folded his arms over his chest. "Come on, man. What's the reason for all the secrecy? You moved back home almost two years ago. You can't possibly have been without a woman all this time."

"I'll tell you what I always tell you. Stop worrying about me and worry about your wife and kids."

"Damn, that reminds me." Gavin pushed back from the table and grabbed his jacket from the back of the chair. "I was supposed to meet Terri at a specialty store downtown to look at some furniture."

"Like I said, worry about your wife and kids," Xavier said.

Gavin's phone rang at that very moment. He looked at the screen and grimaced before he answered. "Hey, baby, I'm on my way. Leaving now," he said, striding toward the door.

Xavier chuckled and shook his head.

"What's going on at the new house?" Trenton asked.

"The renovations are pretty much finished. The contractors are putting down the wood floors in the meditation room this weekend." Xavier wrote a note on the edge of a sheet of paper.

Initially, when he moved back home for good, he had stayed with their mother. A few months ago he found the perfect home—a multi-acre property with plenty of greenspace, set on a hilltop with a clear view of Elliott Bay.

"Good for you."

An odd note in his brother's voice made Xavier look up. He studied Trenton's frowning face as he stared at the table. Guessing his brother needed to talk, Xavier asked, "How are things going with the wedding?"

Trenton sighed. "How are things *not* going, you mean? I swear, if I could run off to Vegas, I would. Between Mother, Lana, and my future mother-in-law, I'm about to lose my mind. The next time Lana asks me a question, I'm tempted to say I don't care, do what you want."

Xavier laughed and set the documents on the table, giving his younger brother his undivided attention. "That will not go over well."

Trenton tapped his pen on the table. "Every time I turn around, there's a wedding emergency. Two days ago, a few people who'd originally RSVP'd they couldn't attend updated their answer, and are now coming. The calligrapher sent over the place cards, but two of the names were misspelled. You'd think the world was coming to an end. One time I got chewed out because Lana ordered eggshell-white linens, but the vendor sent bone-white. I couldn't tell the difference and somehow, that makes me an asshole."

Xavier laughed even harder.

"Why do they even ask me questions? They decide between the three of them anyway. My opinion doesn't mean a thing."

Xavier shrugged. "They're paying you a courtesy. You are one half of the couple getting married."

"I couldn't care less. If it were up to me, I'd show up, get married, eat, and party. Then we would go on our honeymoon. Forget all this extra crap. And to make matters worse, Lana's preparing for finals. May fifteenth can't come soon enough for me." Trenton stood. "When you get married, skip this part."

Xavier grunted. "That's not happening any time soon, so I'm good."

"See you later," Trenton said. He lumbered out of the office.

Xavier packed up his briefcase and glanced at the clock. He'd better leave, too.

He exited the office and stopped at his assistant Jaclyn's door. Through the glass, he saw her working at her desk, with her long braids resting like a high cone on top of her head.

Sticking his head through the gap in the door, he said, "I'm heading out."

She glanced up from the computer screen. "Before you go, I need you to sign something." She picked up a sheet of paper from the side of her desk and rolled her wheelchair over to where he stood.

"What's this?" he asked, taking the sheet of paper and a legal pad she offered for him to press on.

"The letter of recommendation you wanted me to revise," she answered.

One of their employees was moving on to a better position at a chemical company and needed a letter of recommendation. Xavier wished they'd been able to make a place for him.

"Are you still leaving me to go visit your sister?" he asked.

"Afraid so," Jaclyn said.

Her brother-in-law had requested she come stay with them to help take care of the household and four kids while her sister recuperated from surgery, which meant Jaclyn would be gone for a week.

"Are you sure you don't need a temp?" she asked.

"Not necessary. If I need help, I'll call Abigail," Xavier answered, referring to the receptionist who covered the executive floor. He signed the letter and handed it and the pad to her. "Don't stay too late," he said.

"I won't."

He walked out, noting that everyone else in his suite of offices had already left. Normally, he would go through the private elevator reserved for executives if he parked in the executive parking lot, but since he had used a driver today, he went toward the elevator that terminated on the first floor.

As he approached, the doors were closing. "Hold the elevator!" he yelled, sprinting toward the door.

The doors eased back open and he saw Diana inside. He hesitated for a second. The elevator suddenly appeared too small—too confining a space to tolerate such close proximity with this woman. That feeling came over him again—tension in his muscles—joined this time by a lump of heat in his abdomen.

Xavier mentally shoved away the sensations, stepping into the cabin. "You're leaving kind of early, aren't you?"

"Me? No. But I think you are." Did she edge away from him? The doors swished closed.

"This is a little early," Xavier agreed. "I have dinner plans."

"Oh."

They fell quiet. Perhaps it was his imagination, but their conversation felt a little stilted today. Less natural, as if a specter of unease occupied the space between them. He stood in the middle of the elevator, but Diana hugged the corner, staring up at the numbers as if she counted them down in her head.

When the doors opened, Xavier almost let out a sigh of relief. He stepped into the atrium on the first floor.

A few employees loitered nearby, one of them leaning over the guard desk to chat with security. The eerie silence was a direct contrast to the hustle and bustle of staff and guests coming and going during the day.

"I hope my ride hasn't forgotten me," Diana murmured.

"Do you need a ride? If you're stranded, I can call a car for you."

"No, I'm fine. I'm sure he'll be here any minute."

He?

Her eyes looked past Xavier and lit up. "There he is."

She pointed at a man rushing toward them with a harried expression on his face. A full beard covered his chin and jaw, and he wore his hair styled in short, neat twists. Xavier couldn't place his vaguely familiar face, but suspected he worked somewhere in the company.

"Sorry, I'm late," he puffed.

"You're not late. You're right on time," Diana said. "Xavier, this is Bryant Wheeler. He works in the QC department. Bryant, Xavier Johnson."

"I know exactly who you are. Good evening, sir." Bryant extended his hand.

"Good evening."

Bryant winced when Xavier shook his hand much harder than necessary.

"I better get out of here. You two have a good night." Xavier walked away, rolling his neck, jaw unnaturally tight.

He took the cement steps down to the cobalt blue hybrid SUV waiting for him. Once ensconced in the back, his eyes were drawn to the couple as they walked to Bryant's car, but his gaze idled on Diana.

What was she doing with this guy? She'd only been divorced a year.

"Where to, Xavier? Going home?"

His gaze shifted to Cliff's dark eyes reflected in the rearview mirror. Most days Xavier drove himself, but he liked the occasional convenience of having someone take the wheel so he could work. Cliff was his preferred driver whenever he contracted through the car service.

"Change of plans tonight. I'm going to Agua for dinner." He flipped open his briefcase and removed a file for review.

Cliff pulled away from the curb, and as they drove by, Xavier glanced at Diana, watching the friendly, open way she interacted with Bryant as they stood outside his gray car.

Envy churned in his stomach. Grinding his teeth, Xavier fought back the surge of jealousy at the sight of her with another man.

He snapped his attention to the file in his hand. He had no right to be jealous. He needed to get himself under control.

Bad things happened when he lost control.

CHAPTER FIVE

Bryant flexed his fingers. "Xavier Johnson shook my hand. He's got a really firm grip." As if he'd met a rock star, Bryant's voice sounded low, excited, and awestruck.

Diana snapped the seatbelt into place.

Bryant was a quality control technician, and her position on the top floor with the executives impressed him.

"What's he like?" Bryant asked, starting the car.

"He's nice," Diana replied. She couldn't help adding, "And very smart."

One year into his role as COO, *Forbes* featured him on their cover in a plain T-shirt and jeans, the sleeves of the shirt puckered and straining against his thick biceps, and his dreadlocks framing either side of his face as they cascaded forward down his chest. They'd called him the anti-executive, playing up the angle that he bucked convention with his appearance, but extolled his great financial mind, filling in readers on his philanthropic activities before joining the family business, and the goals he'd accomplished thus far.

"Thanks for giving me a lift. I appreciate it." Diana had let Camille borrow her car tonight and Bryant had insisted on taking her home.

"My pleasure." He slanted a glance in her direction.

They'd been friends for a while, and she suspected his interest predated her divorce. Since then, he'd become more aggressive in his attention.

To date, she could find no fault with him. He was attentive, considerate, and even had a sense of humor. But she was still feeling him out, unsure she wanted to change her relationship status from *single* to *in a relationship*. After the fiasco her marriage had been, the very thought made her break out in hives.

But lately she'd been thinking her cousin was right. She did need to start dating again. At the very least, she could enjoy a sexual encounter with a man. Was Bryant that man?

Casting a sidelong glance at him, Diana wondered what kind of lover he'd be. Gentle, for sure. Not the way she imagined Xavier. Xavier would tear off her clothes and—

She swiped away the beads of sweat that broke out on her forehead. She needed to get Xavier off the brain.

"Bryant, I have an invitation to Trenton Johnson's wedding. Would you like to attend with me?"

His eyes briefly left the road. "Is that a rhetorical question?"

She laughed. "I'll take that as a yes."

"Take that as a hell, yes!" he said.

They enjoyed a good laugh, and for the rest of the ride discussed work and the upcoming wedding, imagining the guest list must be a who's-who of the rich and famous.

They pulled into her driveway, exited his sedan, and walked to the door.

Diana faced him, slinging her purse higher on her shoulder. "Thanks again, Bryant."

"Like I said, it's my pleasure," he said, sticking one hand in a pocket and straightening his tie with the other. He cleared his throat. "Diana, it's no secret that I really like you. I just want to know if I'm wasting my time. Do you see this going anywhere, because I'm not looking for friendship."

"Oh."

Bryant laughed nervously, shifting from one foot to the other. "I know this is a heavy conversation right out of the gate, and I hope you don't think I'm being too intense."

"No, I don't. I appreciate you being upfront and honest about your expectations."

"I don't have a choice. I turned forty this year, and I'm ready to settle down. I don't want to waste my time in a relationship that's not going anywhere."

"Believe me, I understand." She took a deep breath. "I have to be frank with you...I'm not in a rush to get into another relationship right now. I've only been divorced a short time, and..."

"And?"

"Moving too fast and not getting to know a person well taught me a few lessons," she admitted.

"Listen, I'm not looking to get married next week. I just want to know that we both want the same thing. I'm not out here looking to add notches to my bedpost. Been there, done that."

"You don't want to add notches to your bedpost, but...you do like sex, don't you?"

"Hell, yes! Doesn't everybody?"

Diana laughed lightly. *No, not everybody*, she thought.

"I have a seven-year-old son," she said.

"That's fine. I'd really like to get to know him, when you're comfortable enough to introduce us. So...what do you think?"

"Can I think about it? And if you don't want to attend the wedding with me—"

"Oh no! No matter what your decision, I'm going to that wedding."

"Good." Diana laughed. "Let's get to know each other first and see how things go from there. No labels. Just two friends spending time together?" she suggested hopefully.

Disappointment filled his eyes. He shuffled his feet and kicked a pebble on the ground. "That works for me."

"Thank you." Diana kissed his bearded cheek, and as she was pulling back, the headlights of a vehicle turning into the driveway swept across them. Her stomach sank when she saw the shiny black Cadillac Escalade pull up beside Bryant's car.

Crap. "I think it's best if you leave now," she said.

He glanced over his shoulder. "Is everything okay?"

"That's my ex-husband dropping off my son early, and things could get a little awkward." She sent him a pleading look, and he nodded his understanding.

"I'll see you tomorrow." He squeezed her arm and strolled to his car.

While Bryant backed out the driveway, her ex-husband, Rodrick Cambridge, climbed down from the vehicle in a leather jacket and dark jeans. He glared at her, and Diana barely refrained from rolling her eyes.

He opened the back door and Andre jumped down and raced toward her, eyes bright and excited.

"Mommy, look!" he said. He held up a brand new box of LEGOs.

"Oh my goodness! Don't you have enough of those?" Rodrick always brought him back with a new game or toy.

"You can never have enough LEGOs," her son said.

"Oh, excuse me." She caressed his head and dropped a kiss to his forehead. "Have you eaten?" She guided him inside the two-story house with a hand to his back. Rodrick followed them into the foyer, carrying Andre's book bag.

"Uh-huh. We had Italian."

"Ooh, sounds nice."

"And when the waitress told us about a chocolate brownie dessert with walnuts, I told her I couldn't have any cause I have allergies."

Andre hadn't had a bad allergic reaction to nuts in three years. Since then, every time she noticed the little hives breaking out on his skin, she gave him Benadryl and he would be fine, but she stayed ever vigilant to ensure he didn't have another attack. She also made sure everyone knew he had an allergy to tree nuts.

"Good job." She gave him a high-five. "Go on upstairs and put away your LEGOs and book bag. I'll be up in a bit."

"See you later, champ," Rodrick said. He gave his son a quick hug and then let the boy race up the stairs.

They both kept their eyes trained on his ascent, and when he was safely out of earshot, Rodrick started in on her. "Who was that?"

Diana steeled herself for the forthcoming argument. She hadn't perfected her defense, but she'd gotten better at protecting herself against his angry barbs. "Rod—"

"You didn't waste any time, did you? Or was he one of your boyfriends while we were married?"

"Stop. Just stop. I've told you a thousand times I never cheated on you. But maybe I should have. At least then—"

"At least then you could break your vows like your father did?"

Diana laughed bitterly. "I'm so tired of this same old argument."

"Because you hate the truth," he snarled, his brown face growing even darker in his rage. "What a fine example you're setting for our son. You clearly don't care about Dre or how it looks for him to see other men hanging around and feeling up his mother outside the house."

"He was not feeling me up." Diana kept her voice low. It wouldn't do for them both to lose their tempers and end up in a shouting match. "You happened to arrive when I gave him a peck on the cheek." She set her purse on the table near the door. "He's a friend."

His face twisted into a mask of distaste. "A friend? With your loose morals, I highly doubt that. You're fucking him, aren't you?"

He made the act sound ugly and distasteful. "Would you please not use that word."

"Which word would you prefer that I use? Screwing? Sexing?"

"I would prefer for you to say that we're simply dating."

"Thought he was a friend."

Smug, Rodrick crossed his arms, and Diana hated she'd let the word "dating" slip out. He had her so shaken she couldn't think straight.

"He is a friend."

"Yeah, right. Let me tell you something." He came closer, and Diana bristled. "You're dating, screwing, fucking—I don't care what you call it. At the end of the day, we both know all the nasty things you like to do. You make sure you don't do them in my goddamn house."

"I would never do—"

"You better not. Cause I will kick you out of this house so fast, it would make your head spin. Do you understand me?"

This was the threat he continued to hold over her head, and part of her hated him for it. Rodrick owned the house she lived in, mortgage-free. It was the first house he'd purchased when he started building a real estate portfolio. He offered to let her stay here after the divorce, and all she had to pay was the taxes. It was an offer too good to pass up, but bearing the brunt of Rodrick's constant threat made her long to get her own place.

"I said, do you understand me?"

"Yes," Diana said through gritted teeth. "But you know what? I'm sick and tired of you—"

Rodrick grabbed her wrist and slammed her back against the door. The sudden movement knocked the wind from her lungs, and she stared up at him in shock. She recoiled as he got in her face.

"Think twice before you say whatever you're thinking."

For ten taut, uneasy seconds, they stared at each other. Blood pulsed in Diana's ears. She'd never seen him like this. It seemed the longer they were divorced, the angrier he became. He'd never put his hands on her before, but he'd also never seen her with another man.

Her heart thrumming agitatedly in her chest, Diana mustered enough bravado to respond. "So you can talk to me any way you want, but I have to mince words? Take your hand off of me."

She jerked her wrist, but his fingers only clamped down harder.

"I meant what I said. I won't put up with you having a bunch of men running through *my house*. You want to screw around like you did when we were married, find a cheap motel like all the other whores." His fingers tightened around her wrist, and Diana gritted her teeth against the pain, meeting his anger with a steady gaze.

"Mommy?" The timid, uncertain sound of Andre's voice came from the staircase.

Right away, Rodrick pulled back and turned his attention to their son. "Hey, son. Mommy and Daddy are having a conversation," he explained.

"But Daddy's leaving now," Diana said. She rubbed her throbbing wrist.

Rodrick glanced at her from the corner of his eyes. "Good night, champ. I'll see you later, okay?" He gave Andre a playful salute, which prompted a return salute from the little boy.

Diana edged away from the door, and Rodrick left without another word. When he was gone, such relief flooded her insides that a tear escaped the corner of her eye. She quickly wiped it away, but Andre saw.

"Mommy, are you okay?" he asked, eyes round and filled with worry.

Diana fixed a big smile on her face. "I'm fine. How was your day?" she asked, filling her voice with cheerfulness. She climbed the stairs. "I want to hear all about it."

****

Diana sat on the side of the bed, watching her son sleep. They'd painted the walls of the room a deep blue, the ceiling black, and pasted stickers of stars and the planets on the ceiling. Andre was fascinated with space and she always tried to nurture his interests.

Smoothing a hand over his hair, she smiled at his partially open mouth. His dusky skin carried the same mahogany complexion as hers, but he inherited his father's long, solemn face and thin upper lip. She dropped a kiss to his forehead, and in the deep throes of sleep, he didn't move an inch.

She moved quietly, picking up a truck and an action figure, and placed them in the toy basket in a corner. A pair of shorts that ended up on the floor were tossed into the hamper they lay right next to.

Before she left the room, she stood at the door and took one more look at him. Her little angel. Definitely the best part of her marriage, and more than worth every fight and painful barb she suffered.

Diana quietly closed the door and went to her bedroom. She dropped her shoes on the closet floor before peeling off her clothes. She stared at her reflection in the floor length mirror, running her hands over her ample breasts in the lacy black bra, over the curve in her thick waist, and down to the matching hipster panties.

Marriage to Rodrick had been awful, right from the beginning. On their wedding night, he hadn't touched her. In fact, their honeymoon had been comprised solely of sight-seeing tours and long days by the pool. No sex. Only after several uncomfortably tense conversations which resulted in her begging him to explain what was wrong, did they finally have sex.

After some research, she suspected he suffered from sexual aversion disorder, and sympathized, worried some traumatic event had influenced his behavior. She suggested therapy, but he refused to go. It took months for them to consummate their marriage, and all they did was go through the motions. They did not make love. Afterward, there was no post-coital cuddling, and Rodrick had rushed into the bathroom and washed the stench of sex off of him. That's how they continued until she became pregnant.

Diana pulled on an oversized nightshirt and climbed into bed.

She endured a sexless marriage for years, not wanting to leave and break up her small family. She'd taken the vows for better or worse to heart and believed they could overcome this obstacle.

But Rodrick viewed sex solely as a means for procreation, and once she became pregnant with Andre, there was no further need for it. Sex for the sake of pleasure—as an expression of love or for enjoyment—was not a consideration for him, and she got little satisfaction from sex toys. You couldn't kiss a vibrator. It didn't hold you afterward.

And that's what she wanted. To be kissed, made love to, and held afterward.

CHAPTER SIX

Xavier never thought this day would come.

At the front of St. Mark's Episcopal Church in Seattle, he stood with his hands crossed in front of him, waiting for the bride's entrance. The Old World style of the cathedral, with its arched ceilings and stained glass windows presented the perfect setting for the wedding ceremony. In what many considered to be the wedding of the year, his youngest brother Trenton was getting married. The billionaire bachelor was getting taken off the market by his best friend, Alannah Bailey.

Xavier stood in line with his two other brothers and four of Trenton's fraternity brothers, all of whom wore white tuxes. Trenton looked dapper in a white tuxedo and a seafoam green cummerbund. On the other side of the altar stood Alannah's seven bridesmaids dressed in one-shoulder dresses in the same shade of green, holding colorful spring bouquets.

Seconds later, the bride's entrance music began and Xavier straightened. The pianist, cellist, and three violinists played a slow, melodious version of "Here Comes the Bride," and the crowd of friends, family, and distinguished guests stood in unison.

Attendants opened the double doors at the back and Alannah was revealed, standing arm in arm with her father—whose brown skin and heavyset frame were in direct contrast to his daughter's smaller frame and amber skin. She looked like a princess in a strapless ball gown with a huge silk organza skirt. The long veil covered her reddish hair, pinned up in a series of curls held in place by a sparkling tiara.

As they slowly approached, Xavier glanced at his brother. A muscle in Trenton's cheek tightened as he looked at his bride. His body remained perfectly still, and his green eyes were shiny with what looked suspiciously like tears.

When Alannah and her father arrived at the altar, she and Trenton couldn't take their eyes off each other. Her eyes glistened with tears, and she blinked rapidly as her petite mother approached and joined them at the altar.

The Episcopal priest asked the parents, "Do you give your blessing and support to the union of this couple?"

"We do," both parents said.

The priest nodded, and each parent kissed one of Alannah's cheeks before taking a seat on the front pew. Alannah and Trenton stood beside each other, and the ceremony commenced. It included a prayer, as well as the call for anyone who thought the couple should not be joined together. During that moment, Xavier held his breath, hoping none of Trenton's exes had managed to bypass security with the intention of spoiling the ceremony. No such scandal occurred, and he breathed easier.

At the end, Trenton and Alannah kissed, and when they stopped, they were both beaming. For as long as he'd known Alannah, these two had been close, and marriage was a fitting end to their friendship.

****

The happy couple had taken dance lessons and first slow-danced to a waltz played by an orchestra in the Great Hall. Alannah had changed into another strapless dress, this one covered in lace with a wide seafoam band around her small waist. While they'd danced, Trenton with his head bent low and Alannah resting her cheek against his shoulder, they'd looked like they never wanted to let each other go, and Xavier was pretty sure that was the case.

Hours later, the party was in full swing. Servers walked around in tails and white gloves, making sure guests had plenty to eat and drink. The internationally-known deejay, flown in for the occasion, played a mix of hip-hop and R&B that kept the guests on their feet or swaying in the chairs.

Xavier circled behind one of the videographers filming the unfolding spectacle. Trenton and a train of his Kappa Alpha Sigma brothers slid onto the dancefloor in a Kappa Alpha Sigma stroll, dancing in front of his new bride and a host of female admirers. Trenton's jacket and tie were long gone, replaced with a huge smile and adoring eyes that seldom left his wife, even as he and his brothers alternated between shoulder shimmies and suggestive pelvic thrusts.

Xavier lifted a glass of champagne to his lips. This was exactly what Trenton had wanted and what a reception should be—a celebration as the happy couple embarked on their new life together.

"Your mother and your aunt are going to faint."

The comment came from Gavin's wife, Terri—Alannah's best friend and matron of honor. Her waist thick with child, she wore the maternity version of the bridesmaid dress, and the same diamond earrings and a necklace with a diamond pendant Alannah had gifted to each woman. Her hair had been pulled back into a chignon like the other bridesmaids.

Xavier's gaze shifted in search of his mother and landed instead on Diana's beaming face. His gaze repeatedly found her during the reception. At the moment, she leaned closer to her companion, Bryant, and he whispered in her ear, prompting her to nod and tilt her head back in laughter. Xavier saw red, jaw damn near locking up as he watched the exchange.

He continued searching the venue for his mother, Constance Johnson, and saw her standing across the room with his aunt, Sylvie. Both women had schooled their faces into composed expressions, but he recognized the disapproval in their countenance.

"Mother does look a bit concerned," Xavier observed, chuckling.

When Trenton and his fraternity brothers wagged their tongues in unison and pumped their hips, Sylvie's eyes widened and she pressed a hand over her chest.

Terri giggled. "Oh my goodness, she's definitely going to pass out."

Gavin walked up.

"Are you going to put a stop to this?" Terri asked, gesturing with a hand and taking his with the other.

A teasing light entered Gavin's eyes as he slid an arm across his wife's shoulder and looked down at her. "Why should I? Cyrus will make sure none of those photos get sent to the press. But hell, this is Trent's wedding day. He's allowed to let loose and enjoy himself. So is Alannah, for that matter."

"True. My girl put in some work to have the perfect wedding. Lord, it was stressful," Terri said.

Xavier's attention migrated to another point in the room, where Gavin's twin Ivy and her fiancé, Lucas, spoke earnestly with each other, their heads close together. He frowned, immediately on alert.

Before he could comment to Gavin, Ivy rushed toward them, her face a cross between fear and excitement. She looked ready to burst, while Lucas's face was drawn into firm, taut lines.

"What's the matter?" Gavin asked.

"It's happened," Ivy said breathlessly. As one of Alannah's bridesmaids, she wore the same jewelry and seafoam uniform. "It's finally happened. We got the call from Cyrus's guy. They found Lucas's mother in Panama."

The declaration shocked them all into silence. Ever since Lucas and Ivy's reconciliation, Lucas had been searching for his parents. The couple had bought a house and lived together with their daughter, Katie, but Ivy had vowed she would not marry him until they found his parents.

Lucas's bearded face appeared grim, as if he didn't want to get too excited about the news. He rested a hand on Ivy's bare shoulder to calm her energetic response. "We don't know for sure that he found my mother."

Xavier understood his desire to tamp down his excitement. Having never known who he was for all these years, Xavier could well imagine that getting close, only to have the possibility yanked away, could take an emotional toll.

"We're flying to Panama tonight," Ivy said. "It's her. I can feel it." She glanced at Lucas with a reassuring smile, which nudged a faint one from his lips.

"We should wait for the blood test," he said.

Ivy shook her head. "Cyrus's guy is very confident." Ivy looked at them all, her eyes glowing, excited for her fiancé. "Hopefully Alannah and Trent won't mind, but we want to leave now so we can get there and meet her first thing in the morning."

"Shouldn't be a problem at all," Gavin said. "Matter of fact, here comes Trent."

Trenton strolled over, eyes aglow and a thin sheen of perspiration on his face. "What are you guys doing over here? Whatever it is, I know I'm missing out on something juicy."

"We found Lucas's mother. In Panama. We hate to leave you and Alannah, but we're flying out tonight to meet her."

"What? Congrats! I'm happy for you." Trenton clapped Lucas on the shoulder. "Don't worry, Alannah will understand. What are you two still doing here?"

"What do we do about Katie?" Ivy's eyes scanned the room in search of her daughter. "We don't want to take her with us, so—"

"I'll take care of Katie," Terri volunteered. "She loves playing with the twins and they love having her around. You know I don't mind, so I don't want to hear any protesting."

Ivy shot her sister-in-law a grateful look. "You're sure? We don't know how long we'll be gone."

"Absolutely. Katie and I will ride with you to get her belongings, and you can drop us at my house when you leave."

"That's settled, then," Lucas said.

They all hugged Lucas and Ivy and wished them well.

"I'll see you later," Terri said, raising up on her toes to give Gavin a quick kiss. Then she followed Lucas and Ivy across the floor, where they said good-bye to Sylvie and Constance. Constance gave them each a hug and patted Lucas's cheek before they left the venue with Katie.

"So Trent, everything set at the office before you disappear for three weeks?" Gavin asked.

"Of course. Unless it's a dire emergency, I don't want a single phone call from any of you while I'm on my honeymoon." He and Alannah were headed to India because she wanted to see the Taj Mahal. Then they were going to stay at a private villa in a luxury resort overlooking Kamala Beach in Thailand.

The deejay put on a slow song, and Trenton's gaze found Alannah across the room. He slowly backed away from his brothers. "I'm going to have another dance with my wife. And don't worry about a thing. Diana and Skip will have everything covered while I'm gone. We should be fine."

At the mention of Diana's name, Xavier's attention went once again to where she sat.

Ever since the evening they ate burgers together, he'd been hard-pressed to get her off his mind. Just the mention of her name made his gut clench. He could still remember the cute little way she wrinkled her nose and her gorgeous smile.

There was little reason for them to interact in the spacious office. She stayed busy on one end of the building, and he stayed busy on his end. But she was a wealth of information, the way assistants tended to know the inner workings of any company, and unable to help himself, he reached out to her more frequently than before. He called her for the most mundane of reasons and solicited her opinion on a variety of projects, mentally using the excuse that she'd been there longer than him and his own assistant. Even as he did so, he quietly acknowledged the reasons for reaching out had less to do with her efficiency and knowledge and more to do with his attraction to the buxom beauty.

She and Bryant seemed rather cozy, chatting and laughing frequently. As he watched, she pointed toward the bar and stood.

Was that fool about to let her get her own drink?

Sure enough, she headed in that direction in a can't-miss-fuchsia colored dress whose design showed off the fullness of her luscious ass. Sleeveless and with a neckline that arrowed into a modest vee over her large breasts, the bold color flattered the nutmeg tone of her skin.

He tracked her movements as she walked to the bar, gliding with long, graceful strides, so that every step flowed with the ease of a choreographed waltz. Her short natural glimmered under the lights and her ample hips rocked from side to side. As she strutted by one of the male guests, the man swung his head around and cast an appreciative glance in her direction.

Xavier glared at him. Why the hell was he looking at her like that?

Diana didn't notice, continuing to her destination across the room and disappearing into the crowd around the bar.

Realizing he was staring, Xavier sipped his champagne. His gaze glided back to the table she'd left.

"Bryant Wheeler works in your department. What does he do?" he asked Gavin, using an inclination of his head to point out the man.

Gavin frowned. "Let's see…" He snapped his fingers. "Been with the company for four years and works on the QC analysis side, looking at data that comes in from the facilities to make sure we meet our objectives for the low count of organisms in the beer, things like that. If I'm not mistaken, one of my managers said he's interested in moving to the quality assurance side of the department."

"Why hasn't he?"

"There's nothing available at the moment. Why?"

"Just wondering." Xavier took another sip of champagne, watching the activity around him. Dancing, laughing, talking, eating, drinking. So many people in attendance to help Alannah and Trenton celebrate the occasion where they embarked on a life together.

Important figures in attendance. The mayor, a senator, and members of Seattle's wealthy elite. People he could be focused on, yet his eyes were drawn yet again to Diana. He watched her stroll over to the table with a colorful mixed drink in hand, garnished with a slice of strawberry on the edge of the glass.

The corner of his mouth upticked. Something a little bad, no doubt.

He continued to stare, unable to take his eyes off her. Every new interaction with Diana left him feeling the same way.

Restless. Hungry. A tightening in his gut.

He definitely wanted her, ached for her, and was beginning to think he wouldn't be satisfied until he had her.

CHAPTER SEVEN

Diana sipped her drink and scoured the room. Nine years ago, her wedding reception had been quaint in comparison, and she'd told herself if she ever married again, she'd save her money and simply go down to the courthouse. Yet she couldn't help but be impressed by the extravagance on display.

The Great Hall had been transformed into a dreamlike setting fit for a king and queen, and the whole room seemed to sparkle. Gold-rimmed plates and matching cutlery sat on each table. Tall white centerpieces stretched upward from crystal vases, and overhead, thousands of glows had been installed in the dark ceiling, giving guests the illusion that they dined under the stars.

Cynthia, one of Ivy's best friends and her executive assistant, sat down with two cupcakes on a plate.

"Where did you get those? When I went to get a drink at the bar, I heard a couple of people talking about how great the cupcakes are."

"Over there." Cynthia pointed across the room to a table against the wall. "They were donated to the wedding party as a way to get free publicity for the startup business. Somebody the family knows, I think. They're spiked with different types of wine, and I heard the chocolate with the Cabernet Sauvignon is absolutely to die for." She took a bite of the chocolate and she groaned, bright blue eyes widening. "Oh my. You have to get one of these."

Diana laughed. "You've convinced me." She leaned toward Bryant. "I've got to try at least one of those cupcakes. Do you want one?"

Bryant shook his head. "None for me. I've had my fill of sweets with the wedding cake, so I'll leave you to that. Hurry back."

"I will." Diana strolled toward the table.

A small sign on the dessert table stated *Compliments of Machmann's Bakery*, with the cake choices segregated into sections marked with little gold signage, listing the type of wine infused in each. Sadly, the Cabernet Sauvignon-infused section of the tray was empty.

Diana pursed her lips and stared at the other options—red velvet, vanilla, lemon, and mudslide. They all looked delicious, but her heart had been set on the chocolate with chocolate icing, and now she couldn't decide.

"Which one are you getting?"

Her heart leapt into her throat and goose flesh pimpled her arm. That deep, sexy bass could only belong to one person. She turned to acknowledge the familiar voice and came face-to-face—or rather, face to chin—with Xavier.

"They all look good, but the cake I want is already gone. Now I'm not sure which one to get."

"And which one is that?"

Diana licked her dry lips. "The chocolate cake with chocolate icing, infused with Cabernet Sauvignon."

"Hmm. That sounds good. Now you have me curious about it." His gaze swept the table of choices.

"From what I understand it's the best of the batch," Diana said.

As he examined the selection, she slid a glance at his imposing form. His toasty brown skin was smooth and blemish-free, popping against the white tux. His dreadlocks were confined to a man bun at the nape, leaving his square jaw exposed in a display and strength and masculinity.

"This one might have to do for me. Says it's infused with Riesling." One large hand picked up a red velvet cake with buttercream frosting.

"That does look good," Diana said. She picked up one for herself.

"There you go, being bad again."

She laughed, her skin tingling all over. "You, too. Although my real weakness is cheesecake."

He lifted a brow. "Really?"

"Mhmm. That's my favorite dessert. I go all the time to this neat little cheesecake shop where all they serve is different varieties of cheesecake. You can go in there and order a coffee or drink, and have a dessert. The owner, Nan, is a doll. She could give you a recommendation of the top sellers, but in my opinion, all the options are *divine*."

"Still, you must have a favorite."

She thought for a minute. "It's hard to decide. Between the Oreo chocolate surprise and the lemon raspberry, for sure."

"Chocolate and Oreo sounds like it might be too sweet for me, but the lemon raspberry sounds good."

"Trust me, it's delicious."

"I believe you."

He bit into the cake, cream-colored icing getting pulled between full mahogany lips. His pink tongue flicked out to swipe away the icing. Diana stared, the inside of her legs throbbing with awakened desire. Good heavens, what was happening to her?

Xavier licked a crumb from his mouth and sucked cream from his thumb. It was one of the most erotic things she'd ever seen—the way his mouth closed over the finger and he made a quick, sucking sound.

Diana pulled air into her lungs and searched the room to get her mind out of the gutter. Watching him dive into the dessert left her a little short of breath. Did he dive into a woman the same way? Licking and sucking with the same unbridled relish?

Maybe she should go ahead and have sex with Bryant to ease the aching hunger that threatened to engulf her. Only one problem.

The erotic sensations she experienced in Xavier's presence didn't overtake her when she watched Bryant eat, or lick his fingers, or…breathe.

"Mm. This is good. I think I'll have another one." He went back to examining the table.

"I better run. I'll see you later." Diana took that moment to escape. She couldn't possibly watch him eat another cupcake. She may orgasm on the spot.

"See you later."

She turned around to acknowledge his words, but froze. Air trapped in her lungs.

Xavier was looking at her ass.

His eyes flicked up to hers. Gaze steady, penetrating. He didn't bother to hide what he was doing at all.

Her whole body heated. She parted her lips to speak, but had no idea what to say. Unsure how to react to his blatant inspection.

Diana started back across the floor, legs less steady than moments before. Did she imagine it? Or had he really been looking at her butt? Was he still looking, watching her walk away with those dark, brooding eyes?

She arrived at the table without collapsing and ignored her cupcake, hardly hearing a word Bryant and Cynthia said.

Her eyes tracked Xavier's panther-like gait across the room. The movement embodied the man himself. Smooth, confident, and very sexy.

He sat beside his mother and propped an ankle to his knee, angling closer to her in conversation.

She continued to watch, drinking in every elegant movement of his body and imagining the sound of his voice as he spoke in low tones. She noted the flash of pristine teeth when he laughed and admired his physical beauty—the long, wide nose and attractive mouth.

Diana swallowed down the lust that threatened to overwhelm her. There was no comparison between both men. Camille was right. Bryant was hamburger and Xavier was filet mignon.

While there were times she enjoyed a good burger, right now, her mouth watered for filet mignon.

CHAPTER EIGHT

His office smelled like leather and patchouli. Earthy. Like the man himself.

Diana stood in the open doorway holding a clear plastic container of lemon raspberry cheesecake. She'd made a special trip to Nan's Cheesecake Shop at lunch and picked up a slice for Xavier.

But this was a bad idea. Clearly, because it had taken her until this late hour to muster up the courage to bring the gift, and her stomach hadn't stopped quivering the entire walk here. When she'd breezed by Jaclyn's empty office, the sensation only magnified with each step she took closer to him.

His head bent over an open book, Xavier stood with his back to her in front of a cherrywood bookcase that took up half the wall, filled with leather bound volumes, business books, and a variety of wood-carved knickknacks that looked like souvenirs from his travels—wooden bowls, a woven basket, and the flags of different countries in a shadowbox frame. He'd removed his jacket and a navy vest hugged his fit body over an off-white shirt.

Biting her lip in indecision, Diana lifted her chin and entered the office. "Knock, knock."

Xavier looked up. "Hey there." Goodness, he even looked sexy wearing those metal-framed glasses.

Diana came within feet of him. "This is going to sound crazy, but I happened to go by the cheesecake shop at lunch and remembered you thought the lemon raspberry cheesecake might be good. After I'd sung the shop's praises so much, I had to bring you a slice." She extended the container.

An eyebrow lifted higher and he slapped the book closed. "Thank you." He took the box.

"Well, that's it. I hope you enjoy it."

What must he be thinking? He could buy his own damn cheesecake. What had *she* been thinking? Mortified, she turned to escape, but his next words stopped her in her tracks.

"Great minds think alike."

When she frowned, he walked over to his desk, and her eyes focused on the way the tailored blue pants sat perfectly on his firm backside.

Setting down the book and cake, he pulled open the top drawer of his desk and lifted out a white box. He walked over and extended it to her.

"What's this?" Diana asked.

"Open and find out."

She opened the box, and nestled inside were four chocolate cupcakes with chocolate icing. Her eyes flicked back up to his face. "Don't tell me this is chocolate infused with Cabernet Sauvignon."

"I think you know the answer to that question," he said, amusement in his eyes.

She wanted to hug him, but that would be completely inappropriate, so Diana settled for hugging the box to her chest instead. "I'll savor these later, maybe with a glass of wine. Four cupcakes. You've absolutely ruined me, but I do believe that I'm up to the challenge."

"So you're not going to share?"

"Maybe one, with my cousin."

He laughed, revealing his pristine, snow-white teeth. "You're a good woman. I'm definitely not sharing even a bite of my cheesecake."

"Once you try it, you won't want to. Trust me." She swallowed in an effort to calm her racing heart. At least the butterflies had disappeared. "Thank you."

"You're welcome. And thank you, for thinking of me."

His warm eyes remained on her face, like a caress, and made heat rise in Diana's neck. "Thank you for thinking of me, too," she said quietly.

His eyes became thoughtful, as if there was something else he wanted to say. Diana wanted him to say it, whatever it was.

When the silence between them extended so long it became awkward, she said, "I'll head back to my side of the office." She didn't move.

Xavier rested his butt against the edge of the desk, crossed his arms, and crossed his legs at the ankles. "If you don't have to rush home to your son, you're welcome to join me for an absolutely bad-for-you dinner."

"Oh? What did you have in mind?" Her heart started racing again at the thought of spending more time with him. Alone.

"I ordered a pizza and told the guards to let me know when it arrived."

"What's on it?"

"All meat. Is there any other kind?"

She laughed. "No, I don't believe there is."

"So, what do you say? Meat pizza and cake sounds like a good way to end the day, don't you think? Let me ruin you some more." His voice dropped a little at the end.

The butterflies in her stomach went berserk at the suggestive comment. "That sounds like a great idea. I'm working in the big conference room."

"Perfect. I'll come get you when the pizza gets here."

Diana walked across the carpet and glanced back as she reached the doorway. He was in the same position, ankles and arms crossed, staring at her. The intensity in his eyes called to some primitive part of her being. She wasn't misreading that heated stare. Not this time. Feminine awareness stirred inside of her, manifesting as a tingling sensation that worked through her veins to the extremities of her fingers and toes.

They both knew what they were doing. What was happening between them. The attraction that simmered below the surface edged toward the boiling point.

Diana sent a faint smile in his direction before continuing the march into the outer office.

****

Balancing two cans of soda atop the pizza box, Xavier found Diana working in the big conference room, as she said. He stood outside, watching her through the glass.

From her vantage point, she couldn't see him because her head was turned slightly away from the door. He, however, could see every delectable inch of her in the black-and-white polka dot dress. A very feminine dress, ruffled along the neckline with a few buttons at the top that fastened over her bodacious breasts, giving enough of a hint of cleavage to make his mind go off on a tangent—wondering what her breasts would feel like when he cupped their weight in his hands.

She bent over the table, palms flat, studying the documents spread out in low stacks on the wood surface. The skirt of the dress hung flatteringly against her shape, doing nothing to hide her womanly curves.

He'd always had a healthy sexual appetite, but nothing he'd experienced in the past prepared him for the pull toward Diana. What would she do, he wondered, if he were to step behind her and press himself against her ass? Would she arch her back and lift her hips against him?

Xavier stifled a groan and ran a hand over his face. He recognized the precarious nature of their interaction. They worked together, and he held a high-ranking position in the firm. He had to tread carefully.

Give her the pizza and walk away, he told himself. It was the right thing to do. The good and safe thing to do.

But deep down, he knew that the right option was really not an option at all.

He pushed open the door and Diana looked up.

"That smells delicious," she said.

56

Good Behavior

She moved the paperwork out of the way, clearing a spot for the box and their drinks, and they both pulled up chairs and dug in.

The conversation remained on neutral ground. First they both praised the deliciousness of the pizza, washing down the greasy goodness with the canned sodas. Then Xavier listened to her talk about her son, Andre.

"That kid is a character, I tell you. The other day, he told me about his 'hidden' talent." She did air quotes with her fingers.

"Oh really?" Xavier set down a half-eaten slice and wiped his hands on a napkin.

It was obvious how much she adored Andre. In the typical mommy way, but also in a way that suggested he was more than the center of her world. She didn't only express the fact that he brought her joy and made her laugh. He sensed a deeper connection, evident in the ethereal, reverential tone of her voice.

"My son informed me he has a very special way to say his ABCs." She shook her head. "He then proceeded to burp the alphabet."

Xavier burst out laughing. "Tell me you're kidding."

"I wish I were. My seven-year-old's hidden talent is that he can burp the alphabet without stopping. He got a big kick out of showing me his skills."

"Did you manage to keep a straight face?" Xavier sipped his soda.

He loved watching her and listening to her. Smooth brown skin, round face, and the dimple on display. She exuded warmth, and her natural beauty was refreshing when so many people succumbed to unnatural ways to enhance their looks.

"I tried to keep a straight face. I really did, but I ended up laughing so hard, by the time he got to the letter Z, there were tears on my cheeks."

"At least he knows the alphabet." Xavier chuckled and set the can on the table near the open box. "What about you? Do you have a hidden talent?"

"No."

She took a second too long before she shook her head vehemently, which made Xavier think she wasn't telling him the whole truth.

"You're hiding something. A young man that talented must get his skills from somewhere."

Her eyes widened. "I do *not* burp the alphabet."

He threw up his hands defensively. "I didn't say you did, but I know there's something."

She pursed her lips, setting her mouth into a full moue that was thoughtful and provocative at the same time.

"I don't tell a lot of people this," she began slowly. "I used to be a band geek. I can play the hell out of the flute."

A moment of silence, and then Xavier burst out laughing.

"Wait a minute, I bare my soul and this is the response? I can't believe you're laughing at me!" Diana tossed a crumbled napkin at him, and it landed in his lap.

"I'm sorry," Xavier said. He set the napkin on the table. "I've never heard anyone use those words in succession. 'Play the hell out of a flute' is not something you hear every day."

"Well, I can."

She pouted, and he wanted to drag her close and kiss her right then.

"I hope I didn't hurt your feelings."

"A little, but I'll get over it," she muttered, picking up a slice of pizza. A smile tugged at the right corner of her mouth.

They ate in silence for a few minutes.

Diana's eyes narrowed. "What about you?"

"What about me?"

"Do you have a hidden talent?"

He hesitated. "Well..."

"You do!"

"Believe me, it's not a big deal."

"Then tell me. And your answer better be better than playing the flute, or I'm laughing my ass off." Her eyes widened and she clapped a hand over her mouth. "I'm so sorry. I got too relaxed."

"Diana." Xavier inclined his body in her direction. Vanilla and coconut filled his nostrils and made his stomach clench. "Do you really think I care that you cursed? It's after hours, and we're having fun. I won't write you up, and I promise, I've heard much worse from the executives I work closely with."

Her shoulders relaxed.

"It's okay to be yourself."

"Being yourself isn't always the best way to go through life." Her thoughts were clearly elsewhere. She plucked a piece of ham from the pizza and popped it in her mouth.

"Who else can you be but yourself?" Xavier asked.

"I guess whoever people want you to be or whoever makes it easier for you."

He studied the forlorn expression on her face. "You can't really be happy if you're constantly concerned about what others think."

Diana pasted a falsely bright smile on her face. "So what's your hidden talent?" she asked, shutting down the heavy conversation.

Because he wanted to see her smiling again—a real smile—Xavier admitted, "I juggle."

Her eyes widened. "What?"

"You heard me." He looked around the room and spotted the perfect objects to show off his skills. He went to the credenza and picked up a paperweight and two coffee mugs turned upside down on a tray.

He tossed the objects in the air, easily alternating between catch and release as he walked over to where Diana sat.

She squealed. "Oh. My. Goodness." She covered her mouth with both hands, eyes wide.

"One day I went to a birthday party, and the clown was juggling, and I was determined to learn how to do it. I practiced and practiced until I mastered it."

"How old were you?"

"Eight. I've been juggling ever since, and it served as a great icebreaker when I went into disenfranchised communities. The kids love it, and even adults find juggling amusing enough that they relax and set aside their reservations. I used my hidden talent to gain their trust." He tossed the cups and paperweight higher, did a complete spin, and caught them all in one graceful swoop.

"Bravo! Bravo!" Diana awarded him with enthusiastic applause. "If the COO thing doesn't work out, you have something to fall back on." She tickled herself so much, she tossed back her head and laughed.

Xavier basked in the aura of lightheartedness emanating from her outburst of laughter. His gaze slid down to her chest, where he had a bird's-eye view of her cleavage—large breasts crowded together in a tempting display of luscious brown mounds. Heat flushed his skin, as if an invisible hand had turned up the thermostat in the room.

He was glad to put a smile on her face again, but what he really wanted, more than anything, was to kiss her.

CHAPTER NINE

Two pieces of pizza sat cold and ignored in the box. Xavier and Diana were winding down, the conversation flowing effortlessly about everything and nothing—planned construction at Pike Place Market, whether or not the office could use a decorative update, and now the *Forbes* article that featured Xavier.

"I didn't want to do the interview," he admitted, "but when *Forbes* calls, you answer, and the story was good publicity for our company."

"And well written."

One of his thick eyebrows quirked upwards. "You read it?" He sounded surprised.

"I did." Diana shrugged. She'd read every word, devouring each bit of detail about him. "It was interesting. Gave good insight into who you are and your vision for the company, but except for your work overseas, not much personal information."

"No, they didn't get too personal."

"Was that on purpose?"

"Yes."

The Johnsons kept as tight a lid as possible on their personal lives, so that wasn't a surprise. She sipped her drink, mustering the courage to ask another question.

"Everyone in the office is curious about whether or not you have a lady friend hidden somewhere." She added a laugh at the end, trying to make light of the comment, but curiosity burned the back of her throat.

"Everyone is curious? Does that include you?" Intense dark eyes watched her closely.

Diana resettled her butt in the chair. "Maybe. A little."

A thoughtful expression entered his eyes. "Between you and me, I've kept my relationships casual over the past year or so. Work has kept me too busy for anything more serious, but I'm definitely the monogamous type. I don't share. Ever."

The last word sounded almost like a threat and sent an unexpected thrill up her spine.

Xavier sipped what must by now be lukewarm soda, and then rested the can on the table. "Since we're getting personal, what about you? You're recently divorced."

"Did you just flip the conversation from you to me?"

"I guess I did." An attractive grin spread across his face, holding her gaze and warming her insides. "But I'm also curious. What happened?"

He sat back in the chair, his legs spread and arms settled on the arm rests. He looked utterly relaxed, but the direction of the conversation made her tense.

Diana let out a little laugh. "My answer is complicated, and to be honest, I'm not sure I should share."

"Why not?"

She shrugged. "I don't know."

"Forget my position in the company. Pretend I'm not Xavier Johnson. Tell me what happened."

She shouldn't. The mess of her marriage was too personal and extremely embarrassing, but in all honesty, she was interested in his reaction. "I can't believe I'm about to do this," Diana muttered, shaking her head. She narrowed her lips and blew out a puff of air. "All right, since you asked, my husband and I didn't last because we were sexually incompatible. I could almost count on my fingers how many times we made love during our eight-year marriage."

Xavier's head bounced back in surprise. "Was the sex bad, or…"

"Um, it wasn't…great, but if that were the only issue, we could have worked through our problem. Our issues went deeper. My ex-husband didn't like sex. At all. He thought it was dirty and unclean. The few times we had sex, it was only in the missionary position." She let out an embarrassed laugh.

Everything about Rodrick reeked of masculinity and virility—from the big car, to the muscular body, to his deep voice. He wore leather jackets and stomped around, aggressive and loud all the time. But it was all a mirage. Overcompensating, perhaps. He hated sex and thought a woman's privates were gross.

"Damn," Xavier murmured, swiping a hand across his mouth. "Only missionary? Nothing else?"

"There were lots of things we didn't do," Diana muttered.

The comment remained in the middle of the room for all of three seconds before Xavier asked, "Like what?"

A hot flush blanketed her neck, and her eyes skirted away from him to the table. "Things I used to enjoy," she answered, purposely vague. She'd already said too much. The conversation was going places it shouldn't.

"What kinds of things could you no longer enjoy because your husband thought sex was dirty?" He spoke quietly but insistently, determined to get an answer.

Diana curled her fingers in her lap, remaining silent. She stared at the table.

"Did he ever…go down on you?"

Diana gasped, her gaze flicking back up to his. Unmasked hunger lay bare in his eyes, leaving her speechless, but she felt compelled to reply and answered past the tightness in her throat. "Never." Her voice came out in a small, whimper-like whisper. "Oral sex repulsed him, and he didn't want me to…offer him…oral, either. He always took a shower immediately after we had sex. Every time. So for him, using our mouths in that way was completely off-limits. We stopped having sex long before we divorced."

Biting a corner of his bottom lip, Xavier's gaze drifted over her, openly assessing her shape. "That's a damn shame."

Diana swallowed. Her body tightened under the scorching heat of his gaze. Her ex-husband had never looked at her like that—as if he aimed to burn the clothes from her body with a simple look.

The only heat she'd ever felt from Rodrick was anger. He insulted her and used harsh words to systemically chip away at her self-confidence and make her feel dirty and ashamed for having a healthy libido. After such a constant barrage of negativity, she began to wonder if the harsh words her husband spewed could possibly hold some truth. Was there something wrong with her for wanting sex more than he did? Did her size really turn him off as he insisted, and if so, why did he marry her in the first place?

"How long has it been?" Xavier asked quietly.

"A long time," Diana said.

"How long?"

The air vibrated with tension.

She met his gaze. "Eight years," Diana answered quietly.

Once her pregnancy was confirmed, Rodrick used to say, *You're a mother now*, as if having a child meant she should completely abandon her sexuality.

Xavier didn't react to her answer in a strong way, but she noticed the slight tightening of his lips. His eyes became hooded as his lids lowered to half-mast. "He must be a damn saint. A woman in the throes of passion is a beautiful sight to behold."

The hunger in the depths of his eyes set her skin ablaze. When his gaze crept past her full bosom to her thighs, she noticed her knees had inched apart on their own. He saw. He knew. She practically propositioned him.

Filled with shame, Diana snapped her legs closed. "I think that—"

His hands landed on the armrests of her chair. Her throat became so constricted, air barely passed through her windpipe. Looking into his eyes, she stopped breathing altogether. Simply gave up.

Xavier wheeled her closer, trapping her with his powerful legs on either side of her thighs. Face to face, neither of them moved.

"Eight years is a long time."

His gaze lowered to her mouth, and tension tightened in the air like the turn of a corkscrew. Diana waited anxiously during his examination, and the seconds ticked by slowly, ever so slowly, allowing the masculine scent of him to seep into her nostrils. She could hardly bear the strain of waiting. Right when she thought she couldn't wait any longer, Xavier leaned in and pressed his mouth to hers.

Shocking. Cataclysmic. Like a burst of energy exploding in the room.

Xavier groaned. So did she.

Binding her arms around his neck, Diana dived in wholeheartedly, allowing his tongue to plunge past her teeth into a sensual sweep of her mouth.

The kiss was devouring. Demanding. Nothing timid or reserved in the way their mouths moved over each other.

"Damn," he muttered, kissing the corner of her lips.

Speechless, anxious, and aching to explore his hard body, Diana lost control of her hands. Fingers clawed at his vest, hands spread over the solid wall of his stone-hard chest.

With an impatient growl, Xavier withdrew and shoved the pizza box to the floor. Then he lifted Diana from the chair and deposited her onto the table. No time to think as he stood between her legs and grabbed her mouth in a hungry, intense kiss.

She clutched at his neck, tilting her head back and allowing his mouth to explore the arch of her throat. He moved to the sensitive shell of her ear. Nibbled on the side of her neck. Every movement—a combination of his soft mouth and the delicate brush of his beard—sent tremors prancing over her skin.

Her clit throbbed, and as if Xavier sensed her need, he pushed her thighs wider and reached under her dress. His fingers slipped beneath the crotch of her panties and she gasped, clinging to his broad shoulders as his thumb flicked the throbbing flesh and explored the wet folds. She swelled and pulsed against his probing fingers, giving herself over to all the sensations he evoked, allowing him to further caress her neck with slow, moist kisses.

He moved upward to her ear, taking his time—as if he savored the taste of her. He touched the lobe with his tongue first, then took it into his mouth and gently sucked on the tender skin. All the while, one hand roamed freely over the curve of her hips and the lift of her butt, while the other continued to rub between her legs. An awful, unbearable pressure filled her loins.

When his hand cupped her breast, she moaned again. That's all she seemed capable of doing. Moaning, whimpering, drowning in the fiery passion of lust. She didn't know why this man or this moment, but Xavier had definitely touched a side of her that had been hidden for too long.

She tightened her arms around his neck and pulled him closer, kissing him fully on the mouth. His lips were neither hard nor soft. They were somewhere in between—perfect. She clung to his neck, their hips seared together as if they'd melded into one. The hard bulge of his erection heated her inner thighs and prepped her for penetration. She readily opened her mouth for his tongue, allowing him to explore and probe and lick the inside of her mouth.

She initiated her own intimate exploration. Nipping his lip. Sucking his tongue. Simply drinking in the dizzying taste of Xavier.

"Oh god," she whimpered, her voice hoarse and raw with longing.

She undid the buttons on his vest and clumsily opened his shirt, exposing his dark skin to her wandering hands. She spread her fingers wide, gliding them over the smooth skin, stopping to graze the nipples with her fingernails.

A tortured groan filled the room, and then Xavier was shoving her dress higher. The lightweight fabric pooled across his forearms as he slid his fingers beneath the sheer panties she wore so he could cup her bottom.

"I've been fantasizing about doing all kinds of things to you," he murmured unsteadily, his eyes dark with hunger.

Diana leaned back onto the palms of her hands as he dragged her to the edge of the table by the knees.

"Against the wall, bent over my desk," he growled.

Then she was in a reclining position, the hard surface of the table beneath her back and Xavier on top of her. Diana held a fistful of his open shirt in each hand, her body bowed off the table. Their lips fused together again, and she kissed him with all the longing and deep-seated hunger in her loins. He nestled comfortably between her legs, his rigid length pressed dead center to her core. As if this was where he belonged.

He grabbed handfuls of her breasts, squeezing them together, rubbing the nipples with his thumbs until her cries of pleasure sounded in the room. His mouth explored the swollen crests with kisses and gentle sucking. Writhing beneath him, Diana strained under the weight of unchecked abandon. Clutching the bundle of hair at the back of his head, she anchored her fingers in his dreadlocks, keeping his face pressed to her bosom.

She wanted this man. Right here. Right now. She didn't care what anyone thought, or even what he might think of her. She *needed* him.

Suddenly, Xavier stiffened. He reluctantly withdrew his tongue from her breast and cocked his head. Diana emitted a whimper, feeling bereft as he pulled away from her.

Xavier swore and withdrew even farther, pulling her into a seated position. "Cleaning crew," he rasped.

Diana watched in a daze as he buttoned his shirt, covering the hard, sinewy muscle of his chest. She almost sobbed with disappointment, but the squeaking cleaning cart finally penetrated the sensual haze.

She hopped off the table. With shaky fingers, she rearranged her clothes and self-consciously smoothed a hand over her short hair. What was she thinking, behaving like that? Like the insatiable whore Rodrick had accused her of being.

A female member of the cleaning crew walked by the glass pushing a cart. She waved. They returned the gesture.

When the cleaner had disappeared, Diana sagged against the table.

For a while, silence filled the room. Diana didn't—couldn't look at Xavier.

"Diana—"

"I'm sorry. I don't know what came over me."

He frowned at her. "I initiated contact." He ran a hand over his head and stepped away from her, as if he needed to clear his head. "Listen, what happened here tonight—"

"Was a mistake." What she felt was too much. Too intense. It terrified her.

They stared at each other.

"Is that what you think?" he asked.

No! she wanted to scream. "It can't happen again." Shame burned her cheeks, and she stared at a spot on his chest to avoid any condemnation that might appear in his eyes. She lifted her gaze over the middle button of the vest that covered the powerful chest she'd had the pleasure of running her hands over. "I don't usually behave this way."

"Me, either. I..." His voice trailed off and his jaw hardened. "It won't happen again," he said.

"If you don't mind, I—" Her sight caught the box and pizza discarded on the floor. It illustrated the impatient manner with which they'd groped each other.

"I'll get that," Xavier said.

The awkward silence was almost as unbearable as the pulse of lust that continued to beat between her thighs.

Diana backed away. "Good night, then." She rushed from the room.

CHAPTER TEN

At Johnson Enterprises, supervisor-subordinate relationships are strongly discouraged. In addition to potentially sparking complaints of favoritism, they could lead to sexual harassment claims. The U.S. Equal Opportunity Employment Commission (EEOC) defines workplace sexual harassment as unwelcome sexual advances or conduct of a sexual nature which unreasonably interferes with the performance of a person's job or creates an intimidating, hostile, or offensive work environment.

Agitated, Xavier snapped the laptop closed.

Unwanted sexual advances. What about the wanted ones?

Standing from the desk, he stalked over to the window. Rain sprinkled from the sky, draping a thin curtain of haze over the sunny day.

He rubbed a hand down his face. Ten days later and his body still burned for Diana. She'd been so wet, had it not been for the cleaning lady, he would have unzipped and taken her on top of the conference table. Now he was looking for a loophole to justify his conduct.

A sudden knock on the door made him start guiltily. "Come in."

Gavin entered. "We have a problem." He shut the door and crossed the room with a folder in hand. "You're not going to believe this, or maybe you will." He placed the folder on the desk. "I know the audit is almost over, but I've found another discrepancy."

"Where?"

"I was talking to someone on the QC team at Morse Brewing. Did you know they had a fire at the brewery five years ago?"

"No. Nathan never mentioned it."

"They did, which made me think about the conversation we had...what was it, about a month ago? Our conversation kept nagging at me, so I decided to review the quality control reports one more time."

Xavier felt the hair on the back of his neck straighten. "You found something."

Gavin nodded. "I asked the QC manager to send me brewing reports for the past ten years. The year of the fire, Morse Brewing produced the same number of barrels they produced the previous year."

Xavier walked a few feet away, letting the answer sink in. He swung to face his brother. "Couldn't they have increased production to make up for it?"

"Not likely. We could do that, because we have multiple facilities. They only have one brewery where they make beer. I know what you're thinking, and I thought the same thing. It's still possible to make up the difference. So instead of looking at the summary data, I drilled down into the details. The shortfall from shutting down the plant should have shown up somewhere. In the quarterly figures. In the weekly figures. Nothing."

"Which means they doctored the numbers."

"Exactly. Which got me thinking even more. I had a few members of the team analyze the testing reports after the fire. Get this: the numbers remained almost constant. They were perfect. Too perfect. I had one of my guys run an algorithm on the probability of that being the case, and it's pretty much impossible. Our technicians are constantly testing batches to make sure yeast counts and pH levels meet the specifications from our quality assurance team, and we still have problems. For them to have that kind of consistency after a catastrophic event is statistically impossible."

Xavier went to his laptop and shook it awake. As he clicked around to find the financial files, Gavin came around the desk and stood beside him.

Xavier entered a password and pulled up the financials for Morse Brewing. With a few more clicks, he was no longer looking at the averages and totals, but examining the day-to-day numbers from the time period immediately after the fire. The more he saw, the more enraged he became.

"No dip in revenue. So where did these numbers come from?"

"Shouldn't the auditors have found this?" Gavin asked.

Xavier shook his head. "The auditors examine current year, previous year, and review the trends." He swore viciously and slammed his hand on top of the desk. "They lied to us."

"Because if we had the true figures, it would affect the offer. What should we do? We've spent months working on this deal, and the midwestern location fits into our strategic plan."

"Doctored numbers isn't only a problem for us. Depending on how bad the financial situation really is, Morse Brewing could shut its doors, leaving hundreds of employees out of work." Xavier rubbed his forehead. "We need to talk to Cyrus." He shoved his arms in his jacket and swooped up the folder Gavin brought in.

They went down the hall to Cyrus's suite of offices. His assistant Roxanne, an older black woman, looked up from behind a pair of fuchsia glasses.

"Is he in?" Xavier asked, not breaking stride.

"Yes, go right in," she said.

After a quick knock on the door, Xavier and Gavin entered Cyrus's office. Their older brother swung around from looking out the window. Jacketless and wearing suspenders, he squeezed a tension ball in his right hand. They'd clearly interrupted him in the midst of deep thought.

"What's going on?" Cyrus looked from one to the other.

"Remember I told you I thought there was something wrong with the Morse Brewing acquisition? That I felt it in my gut?" Xavier asked.

"Yes, and I told you I needed more than your feelings to put a stop to this deal. We've done a lot of legwork. You and Gavin have made multiple visits to have meetings, and the brewery will be top-notch once we invest in the necessary improvements. Everything checks out."

"They're hiding something."

At the skepticism on Cyrus's face, Xavier explained what Gavin had uncovered.

Cyrus's nostrils flared. "Unbelievable. Coupled with the auditors' reservations, this deal is beginning to sound extremely risky." His eyes veered away and then came back to them. "What's the difference in valuation of the company?"

"No way to know until we get the real figures," Xavier answered.

Frowning, Cyrus paced the room, his hand squeezing faster around the tension ball. Xavier and Gavin knew better than to interrupt and let him think in silence.

"We could find another brewery," Cyrus said, but by the half-hearted way he made the suggestion, he wasn't sold on the idea.

"We've been working on this acquisition for a while, and frankly, if Morse Brewing is in dire straits, it could mean leaving all those employees jobless. They need us," Xavier said.

Cyrus looked steadily at him. "Johnson Brewing Company isn't a charity, Xavier. That's what the Johnson Foundation is for. We're buying Morse Brewing to make money."

"I know that. But maybe we can make money and—"

Cyrus shook his head. "There's no maybe about it. If there's no money to be made, there's no point in making the purchase."

Bumping heads with Cyrus reminded Xavier of similar interactions with their father. It always came down to money, and moments like this reminded him of how different their management ideologies were.

"You said yourself they're a skilled workforce. We could help them," he said.

"We help them if we can help ourselves." Cyrus set the tension ball on the edge of the desk. "What's going on with accounts receivables?"

"Someone is looking into the accounts," Xavier answered.

"Here's what we'll do—but we have to be careful. Keep digging, investigate, search, *whatever* is necessary to get to the bottom of this." The unspoken implication was that paying someone off was not out of the question.

Xavier nodded his agreement.

"Gavin, same for you," Cyrus said. "I'm not that concerned about their line of beers, but let's run some tests to confirm purchasing the brewery is still a viable option from that perspective." Xavier opened his mouth to argue, but Cyrus cut him off with a raised hand. "We're not sinking millions into a company that may not pay off in the end. It's terrible if the company folds and the employees are out of a job, but that's Nathan's fault. Not ours. When are you going back out there?"

Xavier blew out a frustrated burst of air. "The final site inspection is scheduled for next week."

"We need to alert Ivy and Trenton, and let's keep your findings between the five of us for now." Cyrus tapped a fingertip on the desk. "If our concerns amount to nothing, then we don't jeopardize the deal. If our concerns are valid, we can contain the fallout."

"Sounds good to me," Gavin said.

"I can probably stall Nathan by telling him there's a delay because of the auditors. How much time do you need?" Cyrus asked.

"Ninety days," Xavier answered.

"You have sixty. Find out what's going on and keep me updated."

"We will," Xavier said.

Cyrus sat behind his desk. "Xavier, I don't think you should go back out there by yourself, but I don't think another member of the executive team would be a good idea, either. It might not hurt to take Jaclyn with you this time—someone lower on the food chain who lower-level employees might open up to."

"Jaclyn's out of town next week."

"How about someone on the operations team?"

"That might work, or…" His mind immediately went to Diana. She would be perfect. She knew much of the background of the acquisition because of working on the project with Trenton, and she had the type of warm, friendly personality staff might open up to. But he hadn't spoken to her since that night.

"I have someone in mind," he said to Cyrus.

"Good."

With Gavin right behind him, Xavier left the office, more determined than ever to get to the bottom of what Nathan Morse was hiding.

****

The electronic invite from Xavier stared back at her from the computer screen. A meeting in his office in one hour. The cursor hovered over the *Accept* button for several seconds before Diana clicked it and went back to work.

She could do this. She had self-control.

The memory of kissing Xavier stayed vivid in her mind. She wanted him, and reminding herself of his position in the firm did nothing to alleviate the longing. She still felt his lips on hers. She still experienced the silky texture of his chest beneath her fingers.

Fifty minutes later, she rose from the chair and took a pen and notepad down to his office. The door was ajar, so she knocked and entered. "I'm a little early," she said.

Behind his glasses, his deep, soulful eyes followed her progress across the room. "You're right on time."

Diana settled into the chair, crossed her legs, and prepared to take notes.

Xavier folded his hands atop the desk. "Next week I'm going to Missouri to do some follow-up on closing the deal to purchase Morse Brewing. As you know, Jaclyn won't be here and I'll need assistance on the trip. I'd like you to come with me. Are you working on any major projects right now?"

How could he talk to her like that? As if nothing had happened between them. As if he hadn't fondled her breasts, fingered her, and made her ache long after she arrived home and all through the night.

"Nothing that I can't step away from for a few days." She kept her tone as neutral as his.

"Perfect. I'll need you to come with me and take notes and do a little bit of reconnaissance work, which I'll explain later."

"So it'll just be the two of us?"

"Yes." No emotion in his eyes or voice. "Is that going to be a problem?"

A trip. With Xavier. Alone.

Her heart started to race. "Not at all."

He cleared his throat and removed his glasses, placing them carefully on the desktop. His gaze on her was direct and steady. "We need to address the elephant in the room. This conversation is long overdue. After what happened in the conference room, I need to make sure I don't make you uncomfortable."

Diana swallowed. "You don't," she assured him.

"Are you sure?"

"Yes." He made her want. He made her long for his touch, but he didn't make her uncomfortable.

"We'll be working closely together. I want to assure you there won't be a repeat of what happened that night. I'm not in the habit of…attacking employees."

She should be pleased that he respected her enough to do what—to an outsider—would be the right thing. Making sure she knew what happened between them was a one-time occurrence. But for her, it felt like their connection ended before it even started, and she partially blamed herself. Overcome by guilt afterward, she'd all but pushed him away.

"…I need someone to be my eyes and ears while we're there," Xavier was saying. "Someone who could fit in with the staff. We'll spend one day at the brewery but be out of the office for two days—Monday and Tuesday of next week. Is there any problem at all with you being gone for those days? Any problem leaving Andre with your cousin?"

His consideration of her son only endeared him to her more.

"No. Camille can watch him."

"All right, then. We should be all set. Please work on the itinerary. Arrange for a car to pick you up early on Monday morning. We'll take the company jet at seven."

Diana grimaced. "That's early."

"With the time difference, we need to strike out early so we can arrive in St. Louis by lunchtime, which is when I have my first meeting. I'll email the list of contacts, addresses, and other information. Any questions?"

"None."

"I'll see you bright and early next Monday then."

Diana rose from the chair and walked across the room. At the door, she paused and turned around, thinking about what her cousin said to her weeks ago.

Well behaved women seldom get what they want.

Xavier had slipped back on his glasses and directed his gaze to the computer screen.

"Xavier." She could barely hear her own voice over the rapid beating of her heart.

"Yes?"

Palms sweaty and heart thumping at an outrageous rate, Diana said, "I didn't feel attacked." That was as bold as she dared be. Did he understand what she was saying?

The air in the room went still. Neither moved, and only the trickling water in the tabletop fountain could be heard.

Without saying another word, Diana quietly left.

CHAPTER ELEVEN

"One million," Xavier said into the phone. He sat in the company jet, a six-seater with fully reclining, extra wide white leather seats. His personal financial manager was on the other end of the line.

"One million to Protect the Rainforest Association and five hundred thousand to Feeding America?" she asked.

"That's right."

His eyes trained on the chauffeured car carrying Diana, which had pulled onto the tarmac seconds before. The driver exited and opened the door. She stepped out in another polka dot dress, this one red with black dots. He salivated, recalling the last time she'd worn polka dots.

"Do you still want me to increase the donation to the Johnson Foundation by twenty-percent this quarter?"

"Yes, and earmark the money for children's programs," Xavier answered, eyes fixed with laserlike precision on how the fabric of the dress hugged Diana's hips and breasts, so that his eyes could do nothing but linger on the ripeness of her shape.

"All right, I'll disburse these funds immediately. Have a safe trip and we'll talk when you get back."

Xavier hung up and stood to greet Diana when she entered. "Good morning," he said.

She returned the greeting. Seeming a little bit on edge, she sat across from him and smoothed her hands over her thick thighs as she surveyed the interior of the plane.

During the flight, they reviewed information about the company. Diana already knew the key players of Morse Brewing, so she was well prepared. Xavier instructed her to talk to the staff, particularly the office personnel, about work conditions and any complaints they had. He knew they'd be more forthcoming with her than with him.

When they landed, a hired car took them to the hotel, and while Diana checked them in, Xavier made a few phone calls. Their interactions remained cool and calm. Very businesslike. Almost distant.

Later, they arrived at the brewery, a sprawling campus on the outskirts of the city, and met with Nathan Morse, the oldest sibling and president of the company. Dark-haired and with clear brown eyes, he greeted them with enthusiastic handshakes.

"Welcome back." He fell into step beside Xavier as they strolled down the hallway. Diana followed behind with Nathan's assistant. "I was surprised when I learned you were coming back."

"This is simply a formality." They didn't normally do a final walk-through of a facility, but due to the sheer size of this transaction, Xavier deemed it necessary to make one more visit. "By the way, I'm sure you talked to Cyrus about the delay with the auditors. We hope to have the final report completed soon."

"There's not a problem, I hope?"

Xavier shrugged, keeping his response casual. "We're at the mercy of the auditors at this point. Until we receive that report, we'll take one more shot at kicking the tires, so to speak."

Nathan nodded vigorously. "No problem." He rubbed his palm across the wall outside his office. "I'm going to miss this place."

"Lots of memories, I'm sure." For the employees, as well. Employees Nathan didn't seem to care anything about.

"Lots and lots of memories," Nathan confirmed. "All right. Let's get to it." He rubbed his hands together. "Anything in particular you want to see?"

"A little bit of everything. After lunch, I'd like to check inventory levels and another quick tour of the brewery would be good."

They ate lunch in the brewery pub, with the employees' eyes drifting in their direction often over the course of the meal. Diana then mingled with the office staff, and Xavier toured the facility with one of the managers.

The day passed quickly, and by the end, Xavier wasn't so sure the extra trip had been necessary. Inventory levels matched expectations, machinery proved operable, and the same management team remained in place. Nothing amiss. Nothing he could see, at any rate.

Xavier invited Nathan, one of his brothers, and the all-male management team to dinner. The small group filled a private dining room. Johnson Brewing Company picked up the tab for a lavish meal composed of copious amounts of wine, food, and spirits, which meant the group was especially rowdy. Xavier noted that Diana wisely only ordered one glass of wine, the same as he did.

During the course of the night, he watched her interact with the group of males. Tonight's outfit was a bright yellow sleeveless dress and red heels. Casual but provocative, the color drew attention to her figure and the silky smoothness of her bare arms.

Definitely a hit, she generated teasing comments and modest flirtation from a few of the men. Marvin, sitting next to her, leaned in several times to whisper in her ear. Once he even suggested to Xavier that he should leave her behind when he left, to which Xavier responded with a tight smile, "I would never leave someone so valuable behind."

Diana laughed easily, flashing a smile that to the other men was merely friendly, but to him, spoke of sensual promise. Every now and again, she listened in earnest to a particularly compelling conversation and fingered her red beaded necklace, or let her forefinger trail along the side of her neck, following the same path his tongue had traced when he'd held her hostage in the conference room.

There was no way to keep his eyes from straying to her time and again. She simply drew his attention. Her husky, vibrant laughter reflected in her large eyes and made the dimple dent her cheek. The sensual way she pursed her lips, or even the cute manner in which she wrinkled her nose—every movement was part of the irresistible tableau that made her uniquely Diana.

At the end of the evening, Xavier shook hands with Nathan and his brother and the rest of the team before he and Diana took a car back to the hotel. In the dark vehicle, the low-volume sound of a local news station came through the speakers, interrupted every so often by the driver's intermittent throat-clearing.

"How do you think the day went?" Diana asked. She crossed one thigh over the other.

Xavier rested a tight fist on his knee. Watching her cross her legs had officially turned into one of his favorite things to view. "Well, but I didn't get any new information. How did your day go?"

Streetlights flashed across her face as they rolled down the highway.

"One of the clerks was especially talkative at the brewery offices earlier today. She said she was glad that JBC was buying the company. Maybe things would improve."

"Did she say what things?"

"Machines left in disrepair, for one. Lack of on-site cleanup, for another. She griped a lot about the way they managed their processes."

Xavier nodded. "We're aware of those problems." Once JBC took over and corrected them, he expected margins and profitability to improve. "Anything else?"

"Marvin said he felt management had the wrong attitude. As if they could do whatever they wanted with no repercussions. He felt corners had been cut in ways that could negatively affect the company."

"Did he just sound bitter, or do you think there's some credence to his comments?" He waited while she considered the question.

"I believe him. At one point he mumbled something about the receivables, but I couldn't quite understand what he said. It was strange—along the lines of 'my hands are clean. I had no part in that.'"

Loose lips sink ships.

"Interesting," Xavier said. "Did he say anything else? He seemed extra friendly." He tried, but couldn't keep the sour note from creeping into his voice.

She blushed. "He flirted a little bit. Nothing serious."

She might think nothing of Marvin's comment, but Xavier's jaw went rigid.

They fell into silence for the rest of the trip. As they whizzed along the highway, a heaviness invaded Xavier's gut. At the hotel, they shared the elevator with several other guests, but he was acutely conscious of Diana's presence only a few feet away.

The cabin stopped on her floor. "Good night," she said quietly.

"Good night."

She hesitated, glancing at him and remaining on the elevator a little longer than needed before she finally exited. The doors slid closed on her voluptuous figure disappearing down the hall, each step in her red heels taking her farther and farther away from him.

Xavier let himself into the presidential suite, sumptuous accommodations laid out like an apartment, with unique artwork on the walls, furnishings in gold, chocolate, and burgundy, and an impressive view of the St. Louis skyline. He tossed his jacket to the sofa and removed the leather clasp from his hair, dropping it onto the jacket with an agitated flick of the wrist.

He had two choices: stay or leave. It was really that simple.

Standing in front of the French doors, he rolled his neck, staring out the window at the lit buildings.

Stay. That was the right thing to do.

Xavier set up his laptop and went to work. By focusing, he managed to get some work done for a while, but reviewing reports and analyzing spreadsheets was not what he wanted to do. Work had held his attention for years—first, in communities here and around the world in South America, Africa, and Asia and now, as the chief operating officer of Johnson Enterprises. Something else held his attention tonight—*someone* else.

Xavier stood abruptly from the chair.

Normally, meditation settled him, but not even such a calming exercise could eradicate the insistent drumming in his loins. The yellow dress and red heels were like a beacon, inflaming his long held lust for Diana.

He poured himself a two-finger nightcap of Scotch, a nighttime activity he didn't usually indulge in. The liquor burned on the way down his throat, and he slammed the empty glass on the bar top.

He'd tried to be good, but there was no way around it. He wanted her. The need burned within him and pushed aside all caution. She wanted him, too. So why should he deprive himself?

Xavier removed his vest and tugged off his tie. With deft fingers, he opened the first two buttons of his shirt and then swiped the key card from the gleaming surface of the bar where he'd dropped it.

Moments later he stood outside Diana's door, knocking very hard.

The pressure of wanting was building to a crescendo inside him. Bracing his hands at either side of the doorjamb, he waited with tense, aching shoulders and arms. Inside, the lock clicked and the door eased open. Diana stood there in a white hotel robe, looking back at him with her wide, round eyes. She'd removed all her makeup and jewelry, and her feet were bare.

Heat strummed more insistently in his blood.

"Eight years is a long time," he said.

"It is," she agreed, voice sounding soft and hoarse.

Xavier's palm pushed against the door, and she let him in without the slightest amount of resistance.

CHAPTER TWELVE

The door snapped close behind him.

Diana backed slowly across the carpet, with Xavier advancing like a lion stalking prey. His mane lay loose and free down his back, and the top buttons of his shirt were open to reveal the strong column of his throat.

"I don't know how it's possible for a man to live with you and not touch you." The low baritone of his voice was even deeper, and contained a rough, raspy edge.

His fingers stroked down the side of her face, the featherlight touch inflaming her skin. For years she'd ached for contact, longing to be touched and to feel wanted. Diana leaned into his big hand, and closed her eyes for brief seconds before opening them again, only to get lost in the dark depths of his pupils.

Nostrils flaring, his keen brown eyes swept over the robe, practically burning the garment from her body with the heat generated from his gaze. "Give me one night, Diana." He stepped closer, their bodies almost touching, the fierce light of determination in his eyes. "One night, and I'll make you feel better than you've felt in years. I'll have you screaming my name. I'll make your toes curl. All you have to do is tell me how you want it. Gentle or rough? Tell me, Diana. Tell me how to fuck you."

His words turned the dull ache into excruciating agony that left her weak-kneed. "Rough," she whispered.

His mouth came crashing down on hers with urgency. The kiss was hard and unforgiving, as if a trace of anger lay beneath the desire. Diana parted her lips, taking his tongue and tasting the caramel and anise notes of strong liquor.

His big hand cupped the back of her head, fingers sliding over the short curls even as his other hand busied with untangling the knot at her waist. When Xavier had released the belt, he drew back enough so that he could look down at her almost naked body.

"Damn," he whispered, trailing a finger down the middle of her torso.

Perhaps she'd known he would come. Some sixth sense warned her to prepare for his arrival, because her freshly washed skin was bare and lightly scented with vanilla-cream lotion, and only thin black satin hugged her hips.

Xavier offered a glimmer of what her life had been missing for a long time. Excitement. Passion. Intimacy. All she wanted was for him to finish what they'd started at the office and take her against the nearest horizontal surface.

He fastened his lips over one breast, and the immediate dart of pleasure made Diana gasp and curve into his mouth, capturing a handful hair to anchor him to her chest. She liked his locs loose like this. It gave him a leonine appearance and something for her fingers to hold onto.

His tongue played with the tight nipple while his hand lowered down her spine to grab the fullness of her buttocks. He kissed up her breasts to her neck, inhaling deeply when he arrived at the little crater in the middle of her collarbone. His touch already had her spiraling out of control and trembling with need.

"Xavier," she breathed, as he backed her toward the bed.

Soon, they were both stripped bare, with only naked brown skin on display. When she saw the bold manifestation of his erection, between her legs dampened with anticipation, and she almost dropped to her knees to take him in her mouth and taste every inch of his formidable length. But Xavier had other ideas. They lowered onto the cool sheets and he kissed the apples of her cheeks. Trailing his mouth lower, he seared kisses along her chin and the underside of her jaw.

"Your skin is like velvet," he murmured against her throat, the strain in his voice evident as he ran his hands all over her skin.

Kissing and touching, they explored each other's bodies with rough-textured caresses. His sculpted body was smooth to the touch, and made up of chocolate silk poured over hard steel. Her fingertips trailed over his abs and his pecs flexed when they encountered the moist flicker of her tongue.

Exploring him was a delight, and Diana couldn't recall the last time she'd felt so excited. So sexually energized. Everything about him turned her on. The earthy fragrance of his skin. The taut, beautiful lines of muscles covering his body. She poured kisses on his thick neck, his wide chest, and muscular arms—where foreign symbols were etched in black on his biceps and shoulders.

Then he began to explore her. His hands cupped her breasts and squeezed their fullness. He was merciless with his attention, sucking the tips with such avid thoroughness that she writhed beneath him, her body throbbing and begging for relief. Wherever his hands went, his mouth followed.

They smoothed over her stomach, launching a series of faint quakes on her skin. Lower still, his hand slid over the curve of her abdomen. Obediently, his mouth followed, tasting the quivering flesh and teasing with gentle pressure. His hands caressed the flare of her hips and kneaded the tender skin of her inner thighs. Again, his mouth followed. When his palm covered her mound and nestled in the damp hair below, Diana almost exploded right then. She closed her eyes and waited for his mouth to follow.

Instead, Xavier took the belt from the robe and said, "I want to tie you up. There're no bars on the bed, so I'll have to tie your hands behind your back. Are you okay with that?"

"Yes," Diana whispered, near the point of agreeing to anything he suggested.

She turned onto her side and allowed him to bind her wrists. As he tightened the knot, a kernel of fear broke through the sensual fog. He could do almost anything he wanted once he bound her.

"Are you okay?" he asked, testing the binding, his eyes searching hers.

His concern unraveled the fear in her belly. "Yes," she whispered.

"I really wanted you to ride my face, but we'll save that for another time."

He resumed his exploration, stroking his hand in a careless, almost negligent way between her legs. But he was prepping her for what was to come.

He lowered his head and inhaled. "You smell so good." He was so raw. So carnal.

When his head dipped between her legs, her thighs fell apart and she drew in a deep breath before his tongue even touched her heat.

Her fingers curled, the nails biting into the flesh of her palms. Moaning, she whimpered his name, and her enthusiastic response seemed to spur him on. He lifted her ankles to his shoulders and kept his head buried between her legs. He took his time probing the folds, sucking her clit, doing whatever he wanted, as though he couldn't get enough.

Diana struggled against the restraints, but she was helpless and forced to bend to his will. His tongue toyed with her flesh and he held her legs apart, forcing her to take the pleasure, giving her no reprieve against the onslaught of his mouth.

He was the one in control, and he wouldn't let up. No matter how much she panted. No matter how much she pleaded. It was as if he were making up for all the years she'd gone without, and she was so aroused, so wet, her core practically wept for him.

She came. Embarrassingly fast. Waves of pleasure rippled through her body, intensified by the restraint knotted around her wrists. Her breasts juddered with convulsions so deep, so profound, that she rolled onto her side, spent and moaning. He'd released her wrists before she became fully lucid again.

Struggling to regain her breath, Diana took note of the tender way Xavier pressed his lips to the inside of each wrist. There might be bruising tomorrow, but for now she marveled at how gentle and caring he was in the midst of their lovemaking.

His erection was like hard marble against her belly. She reached between them to cup him in her hand, watching his eyes close as she stroked the taut flesh. A bass-toned rumble filled his chest. One of pure, unrestrained, masculine pleasure.

"I need to be inside you," he whispered.

He left the bed and retrieved a condom. When he'd slipped it on, he rejoined her on the mattress and took her mouth once again in a long, probing kiss.

"I know it's been a long time," he whispered.

"I don't care," she whispered. "Just take me, and don't go slow." She hooked her arms behind his neck.

The head of his shaft nudged the entrance to her body. He eased in at first, but she lifted her hips, insistent that he slide all the way in. His pelvis surged forward and her mouth fell open as she took every hard, pulsing inch of him. He glided in and out, the fullness of him stretching her wide, and his length embedded deep within her canal.

"Faster," Diana whispered, drawing one foot to the middle of his back and fastening her hands in his hair.

He withdrew and then refilled her with greater speed.

Her fingers clenched into fists behind his neck. "Harder," she begged, wincing at the pleasure-pain.

Gritting his teeth, Xavier obliged, fulfilling his promise to give it to her rough. An almost feral light entered his eyes. He moved with force. Rocking the bed. Taking her the way she demanded. Savagely. Hard. Without mercy.

Nails sinking into his back, Diana gave herself over to the current of heat that licked at her loins. The orgasm powered through with unparalleled force, more bone-deep than the last, reducing her to nothing but a trembling mass. She cried out his name, her toes curling into tight knots. The gasping sounds of passion that escaped her were loud and foreign in the quiet room.

Seconds later his thrusting stopped and his body stiffened. A faint groan—closer to a growl—left his throat, and he collapsed on top of her. The *throb, throb* of their hearts hammering in a synchronized rhythm echoed in her ears.

Xavier breathed heavily into her neck, the ropelike strands of his hair strewn across her breasts making her sensitive skin tingle.

With a groan, he rolled onto his side and pulled her with him.

CHAPTER THIRTEEN

Sunlight filtered through the window and bathed the knee sticking out from under the duvet in warmth. Diana stretched out the soreness in her muscles, burrowing deeper into the comfortable heat at her back. As consciousness slowly entered her brain, she realized the arm flung across her waist and hard flesh pressing into her spine were unfamiliar sensations. She stiffened.

"Good morning," a husky male voice said behind her.

She'd slept with Xavier. Xavier Johnson. The chief operating officer of Johnson Enterprises.

She closed her eyes.

"How do you feel?" A gentle hand coasted over her hip to her thigh.

Slowly, Diana opened her eyes again. She shifted and winced at the faint throbbing between her legs. "A little sore," she admitted.

"That's to be expected. It's been a long time."

And he'd given her quite a pounding, half killing her with his sensual touch and hard, deep strokes.

Xavier was the male version of a lady in the streets but a freak in the sheets. In his case, a gentleman in the office transformed into a beast in the sheets. He'd given her four orgasms last night. First with his mouth, from the missionary position, from the back—she shivered at the memory—and then tied her arms behind her back and lifted her leg over his shoulder, fitting his body to hers in a scissors position. She was exhausted but very satisfied.

His mouth caressed the nape of her neck and his fingertips ran up her thigh. "You're an incredible woman, you know that?" he whispered.

Diana twisted onto her back so she could look into his eyes. His dreadlocks fell around his shoulders, and she tentatively fingered one. In the light of day, it felt strange to touch him at will.

"You're the one who's incredible. Last night you helped me break a very long dry spell, and I appreciate it."

"It doesn't have to end with last night." Xavier sat up, and the sheet fell away to his hips, exposing the breathtaking terrain of his muscular torso. He eased the sheet lower on her chest, and with her breasts free, he bent his head and sucked the right nipple, turning it instantly hard.

"Xavier," Diana moaned. She pulled away from him and sat up, holding the sheet against her aching breasts. "What do you mean?"

A warm expression caressed his lips and filled his eyes. "We have all day in St. Louis. Why not make the most of it?"

"You have phone calls to make and a meeting with a supplier at ten o'clock," she reminded him.

"I can cancel the meeting and work the calls into the day as we explore the city. I've been here several times, but except for going out to eat, I haven't seen much, and you've never been to St. Louis before."

"You want to go sightseeing?"

"Sure, why not? We could eat breakfast somewhere nearby, go sightseeing, eat lunch, do more sightseeing, and then come back to the hotel for dinner at the private pool at my suite."

She loved the idea of exploring the city, and doing it with Xavier made the excursion sound all the more enticing. "Why are you doing this?"

He paused. "Because I want to," he finally said.

She didn't know what answer she'd expected, but she was slightly disappointed by the one he gave. Diana plucked at the sheet. "Promise me something?"

"Anything."

Her gaze lifted to his. "No judgment, no regrets for the next twenty-four hours. I won't be Diana Cambridge, executive assistant, if you agree to not be Xavier Johnson, COO. And we just enjoy each other, living in the here and now."

"Being bad?" he asked.

"Yes, being bad."

"That's all you want?"

"That's it."

He leaned in. "No problem. We can do that." Xavier kissed her neck, and her loins ached with need for him.

"Are you sure?" Diana whispered, even as she arched her neck so his lips could travel freely over the sensitive skin.

"Whatever makes you feel comfortable." Xavier gently sucked her neck and dropped a kiss to her shoulder. "Now, let's get you fixed up with a warm bath."

Diana cupped his jaw in her hand. Brushing her fingertips over the fine hairs on his face, she looked deeply into his eyes. "Thank you for last night." No matter what happened later, she would be able to hold onto the memory of what they shared.

"Diana," he said gravely, his expression sincere, "making love to you was just as pleasurable for me as it was for you. And remember, we still have twenty-four hours to go."

They walked naked into the bathroom. Diana was so busy ogling him she forgot to be self-conscious about her own nakedness. Her eyes drank in the firm muscles of his buttocks and hamstrings. As if in slow motion, they rippled with each movement under the lights. His back, too, was a sight to behold. Wide and muscular, even now she itched to touch him.

Xavier ran water in the giant tub, and they both climbed in to the hot, bubbly water. With her back to his chest, he gently bathed her, squeezing suds from the washcloth over her breasts, and taking extra care between her legs. Despite the long night of lovemaking and her body's soreness, she still became aroused when he touched her.

By the hard rod pressing into the middle of her back, he wasn't immune, either. But he carefully—dare she say, lovingly—continued to tend to her in the gentlest of ways.

"You have some interesting tattoos." Last night, kissing his back, she'd read the message written in block letters between his shoulders. Diana traced a hand over the decorative symbols on his bicep. "What's the origin of the words on your back, and what are these?"

"*A tree is strong because of its roots* is a Zambian proverb." He ran a hand over the marked flesh on his arm. "These are Adinkra symbols, originated in Ghana and Cote D'Ivoire. They're plenty more, but I chose seven. Each one represents a different concept."

"What do they mean?" Diana asked, tilting her head up to look at him.

Xavier pointed at the first one, right above his elbow. "The *sankofa* represents the importance of learning from the past, something that's come to mean a lot to me as I've gotten older." He laughed softly, in a self-deprecating manner, and pointed at the next in line. "*Wawa aba* symbolizes perseverance. *Okodee Mmowere* are the talons of an eagle and represent strength, bravery, and power."

He went through the entire list of seven, pointing to each in turn and stating the name and what it represented. Then he told her about his trips to Ghana and Cote D'Ivoire, and the differences between those countries and his ancestral home in Senegal.

Listening to the quiet, deep timbre of his voice made Diana feel as if she were getting a civics lesson. He'd taken a little something from each country he visited and didn't treat Africa as a monolith, as so many people tended to do, herself included. He embraced the different cultures of the continent and appreciated the diversity in the people and customs. He made her long to know her own ancestry.

After the bath, Xavier went back to his room to get dressed, but dropped a kiss on her mouth before he slipped through the door. Biting her bottom lip, Diana shook her head. She couldn't believe what was happening.

"Don't overthink it, Diana," she told herself.

She wouldn't, but she couldn't possibly keep last night to herself. She picked up her phone and sent a text to her cousin.

I've been bad.

While waiting for Camille to respond, she pulled on a pair of jeans and a purple blouson top with a wide, figure-hugging banded hem. Purple lipstick followed as her phone vibrated with a reply.

What did you do? Details!!!!

Diana tapped out a response. *I'll tell you everything when I get back.*

Tease!

Diana laughed and slipped on her shoes. *Did Dre get to school okay today?*

Yep. After your convo last night, he went right to sleep. I think he just wanted to hear from you.

Diana's heart warmed. She'd called him later than anticipated, but was glad he was up so they could talk. They'd only talked for a few minutes—enough for her to tell him how much she loved him and wish him a good night's rest.

I'll call earlier tonight.

Later! xoxo

Diana rubbed coconut oil between her palms and massaged it into her hair and scalp. Using a soft-bristled brush, she brushed her hair, finishing up as the sound of a knock filled the room.

She rushed across the carpet and opened the door to Xavier. He appeared refreshingly casual in navy chinos and an off-white ribbed T-shirt that molded to his chest and showed off his firm pecs. His face was cleanly shaven and the scent of lime and menthol from his aftershave filled her nostrils. He wore his hair in a loose man-bun atop his head that allowed several locs to hang loose in the back.

Have mercy! Did she really spend the night with this man?

"You ready?" he asked, one hand braced on the door jamb. His eyes ran down the length of her body, and a wolfish smile lifted the corners of his mouth.

Diana giggled. "You can't look at me like that when we get back to the office."

"Are you planning to wear ugly clothes every day?" he asked.

"No."

"Then we have a problem."

Diana stepped close and boldly reached for one of the loose locs. She twisted the rope-like hair around her finger. "You're definitely good for my ego," she said softly, boldly planting a kiss to his soft mouth.

His hand slipped around to her bottom and pressed her closer. Already, she could feel him hardening against her stomach. "You better behave yourself or I'll forget breakfast and take you back to bed."

"Mmmm." Diana kissed his neck, inhaling the aftershave scent in his skin. "If I weren't hungry, I'd take you up on your offer."

She went back into the room to grab her purse.

"So you'd rather have food than me?" he asked from the doorway.

"Not at all." She strutted back over to him, feeling positively beautiful by the way his eyes watched the sway of her hips. "But I'll make an exception this time."

"Come on. I'm starving, too."

They headed down the hallway.

"How about we go by Anheuser-Busch for one of the sightseeing tours?" she said.

She had never been to St. Louis but knew Anheuser-Busch held the leading share of the U.S. beer market and was headquartered in St. Louis. Like Johnson Brewing Company, they offered guided tours of their facility.

"We'll go there over my dead body," Xavier said. "They're the competition. Unless you're going to the brewery for corporate espionage, the answer is no."

"Oh come on, I think it would be interesting," Diana teased.

Xavier frowned at her. "Hell, no. And don't ask again."

He took her hand, and for two seconds the act surprised her. But then she relaxed into the naturalness of it, and closed her fingers around his bigger hand, letting him lead the way down the hall.

CHAPTER FOURTEEN

They ate a hearty breakfast of big fluffy pancakes, eggs, and bacon at a restaurant recommended by the concierge. Immediately after, they set out, taking advantage of a hop-on, hop-off tour that gave an overview of the city and lots of information. The trolley stopped at popular locations, including the St. Louis Arch, Millionaire's Row, and the Cathedral Basilica, dedicated in 1914 and known for having one of the largest mosaic installations in the Western Hemisphere.

Diana took plenty of pictures and sent a couple of selfies to Camille.

They chose an Italian restaurant for a late lunch, and Xavier knew the perfect spot where they could eat toasted ravioli, a signature St. Louis dish he insisted Diana try. She immediately fell in love. The deep-fried appetizer was stuffed with meat, dusted with Parmesan cheese, and absolutely delicious. They ended the meal with individual orders of gooey butter cake, another favorite in the Gateway City.

Intermittently, Xavier made calls during the day. One in particular lasted thirty minutes, during which she occupied herself browsing at a gift shop. They finished the tour in the late afternoon and went back to the hotel.

"I'm glad we had time to sightsee," Diana said, as they strolled down the quiet hall. They stopped at her door.

"Still up for dinner in my room?" Xavier asked.

She wrinkled her nose. "I'm full from lunch, and I need to check on my son."

He braced one arm over her head against the wall. As usual, he appeared intent on her, offering his undivided attention. She enjoyed being the focal point, something she hadn't experienced in her marriage, and barely restrained from posing or twirling in a circle every time Xavier's gaze landed on her.

"I'm not hungry, either. I'll order something for us to snack on. Do you have a taste for anything in particular?"

Just you, Diana wanted to say. Although she enjoyed the day out, she greatly anticipated spending the evening with him. "Surprise me."

"Your wish is my command." He removed a spare key card from his wallet and handed it to her. "Come in when you're done." He dipped his head and took her mouth in a slow, sensuous kiss. A kiss she felt all the way to her toes. "See you in a few."

Diana lingered in the hall before going into her room, watching his tall, broad frame walk away. Biting her lip, she sighed before entering the room.

When she called Seattle, Camille answered the phone. "I know you called to talk to Dre, but can you at least give me a hint about what's going on with you in St. Louis?"

"No, you'll have to wait." She enjoyed torturing her cousin.

Camille growled in mock anger. "You suck. Here's Dre."

"Love you, cuz."

"Whatever."

Seconds later, she heard, "Hi, Mommy! Are you having fun?"

Diana grinned at his cheerful voice. "I sure am. But I want to hear all about your day."

She lay back on the mattress with the phone pressed to her ear and listened to Andre's recounting of a food fight in the lunchroom, which he swore he didn't participate in. Then he went over his new vocabulary words and mentioned his class ate ice cream to celebrate a friend's birthday.

She was glad they'd eaten ice cream instead of cake. With his nut allergy, she always worried about events like that at school. Even though he knew he couldn't eat just anything, he was still a child and prone to temptation. The teachers were diligent, too, though.

Forty-five minutes had already passed by the time she told him to do his homework and be a good boy for cousin Camille.

Diana freshened her lipstick and double-checked her clothes before leaving for Xavier's room. Using the key card he'd given her, she let herself into the presidential suite.

Her eyes swept the elegantly decorated room. "Xavier?"

She walked across the wood floors, and through the French doors she saw Xavier in the pool. Near the door was a display of snacks—cheese and gourmet crackers, fruit, nuts, hummus, and pita chips. A bottle of white wine chilled in ice, with two glasses next to the bucket.

Diana helped herself to the wine and went out to the pool. Xavier was swimming away from her, and in the fading afternoon light, his skin glistened like mahogany satin, his locs trailing behind him like a herd of snakes. His powerful arms sliced through the water, and she was a little jealous of the water because it got to touch and embrace every inch of him, something she looked forward to doing later.

"I see you found the wine," Xavier called, cruising toward her with even strokes.

"Yes. It's good, too." She took a sip before removing her shoes and rolling up her pants leg. She sat on the edge of the pool and let her feet splay in the cool water.

Xavier came to stand beside her, the water bobbing around his lean waist and droplets snaking down his chest like racing teardrops.

"You should come in," he said, his deep voice tempting her.

Diana laughed. "I didn't bring a suit."

"You don't need one. There's nobody here but you and me."

She eyed him. "You're serious?"

"Of course I'm serious. Come on, woman. Get in."

The next thing she knew, he'd hooked his thumbs in the black swim trunks and removed them. Diana's eyes widened as he tossed the wet shorts onto the cement.

"Now you're not alone," he said.

Diana laughed. "I don't even know who you are."

"Xavier Johnson. Do you know who you are?"

She contemplated the question. In all honesty, for a long time she didn't know who she was. She'd stifled her personality for years, leaning on efficiency and dependability at work to hide the disappointment of her marriage and her own internalized failure as a wife.

"I'm beginning to figure it out," she answered truthfully. "Here goes." She set the wine goblet on the ground and stood up. With Xavier's gaze glued to her, she first removed her top and bra, and then stripped out of her jeans and underwear.

A lupine smile spread across his mouth. "Get in here."

Diana wrapped her arms around her breasts and jumped in. She squealed and squinted when the cool water splashed her face. "You've got me doing all kinds of crazy things."

"I plan to get you to do much more," he said, wading closer to give her a kiss.

They swam around for a while, playfully splashing each other and occasionally kissing and touching as night fell. She couldn't believe how relaxed she'd become with him viewing her body, but Xavier made her feel comfortable in her own skin, sexy and desirable in a way she'd never felt before. And how could she not, when his eyes filled with heat each time he leaned in for a kiss, and he touched her with a combination of reverence and desire that made her feel like the most beautiful woman in the world. A stark difference from the reaction she used to receive from the man she'd married.

After a long time, they finally exited the pool and rinsed off in the shower. Diana helped Xavier wring out and dry his long hair, and then they ordered dinner. She chose a fish meal and Xavier ordered a St. Louis-style ribs dinner. They ate in the dining room of the suite, dressed in the hotel's white robes, drinking wine, and sampling each other's meals.

Later, they made love. Slower, sweeter, more tender this time. He was so tender, Diana almost cried. She didn't want to think about how things would change in the morning. No matter what happened, she'd never forget the past twenty-four hours. In a short time, Xavier had exhumed an aspect of her personality she'd thought long dead.

Because of that, a piece of her heart would always belong to him.

CHAPTER FIFTEEN

She hadn't thought this through.

Diana watched Xavier pace outside the patio doors of the hotel restaurant, a sick feeling in her stomach.

For the flight home he'd chosen a charcoal suit, but the jacket lay on the back of one of the chairs at the table. The vest enveloped his firm torso like an embrace, and the light blue shirt highlighted the richness of his dark brown skin. The neat, ropelike strands of his hair were bound and secure in a dense man bun at the nape.

She'd asked him for twenty-four hours, but realized she wanted more. Much more. And it scared her. Being with Xavier was like having a bright light switched on in a pitch black room. Her sprits lifted. She could see clearly. Now she was expected to go back to darkness. Simply turn off the emotions he evoked. She wasn't an automaton. She didn't operate that way.

Diana pushed the scrambled eggs around on her plate.

"Ma'am, is the food all right?" The server, an older woman with graying hair and a mild manner, had been almost annoyingly attentive. She frowned at the plate filled with eggs, sausage, and toast.

"The food is fine. I'm just not very hungry."

"Can I get you anything else?"

"A little more coffee, please." The woman filled the cup almost to the rim and Diana thanked her. She ate a few bites of sausage and forced herself to swallow the food.

Xavier came back to the table frowning, his jaw rigid.

"Problem?" she asked.

He spread the white napkin across his lap.

"An issue at the Portland facility," he replied in a detached voice. "I might have to go down there, but I hope not."

He gulped down some orange juice and picked up his utensils.

With envy, Diana watched him dive into the food. He'd dived into her body the same way, with gusto and enthusiasm. He'd made her feel treasured and sexy and desired.

Yet he'd sat down at the table, and not once had he looked at her. He'd barely looked at her all morning. From the time she quietly left his suite to now.

No doubt when they returned to Seattle, he'd move on to another woman. Someone from his social circle, perhaps. She wished she could have one last kiss, something to hold her over, but twenty-four hours was all he'd agreed to. It would have to be enough, and it was stupid of her to get attached to this man.

Look at me, she pleaded silently.

He simply continued eating, devouring first the pancakes and then the eggs and bacon. The entire time nausea swirled in her stomach.

Nearing tears, Diana tossed her napkin to the table. "I have to run back to my room to...for something. I'll meet you in the lobby when it's time to leave." She jumped up from the table.

He looked up then, but she swiftly turned away so he couldn't see the despair in her face. She bolted across the dining room floor, charging between the tables and dodging a male server with a tray of plates on his shoulder. She marched down the first floor hall to the ladies' bathroom and barely made it into a stall before the limited contents of her stomach came up.

Kneeling on the cold tile, tears streamed down her face. Diana wiped them away with a shaky hand. What was happening to her? She had to learn to contain her emotions. She'd done it for years with Rodrick. Surely she could manage the flight to Seattle after two measly nights with Xavier.

She stumbled out to the mirror and checked her face and washed out her mouth. Bracing her hands on the counter, Diana gave herself a pep talk. She could do this. She was Diana Cambridge—efficient, professional.

Straightening her blouse, she left the bathroom.

Thirty minutes later, a car picked them up from the front of the hotel. The flight back to Seattle was held mostly in silence. Xavier spent the entire flight alternating between his laptop and the phone. Diana reclined in one of the white leather chairs and pretended to sleep.

When they arrived at the airport, two cars waited. Xavier's cobalt blue SUV with his personal driver, and a hired car for her.

"I'll see you at the office," she said to him. The wind fluttered her skirt as she walked briskly away, dragging her wheeled suitcase behind her.

Blinking rapidly, she practically dived into the car. When the driver pulled away, she couldn't bring herself to look back. It was over. Twenty-four hours. No regrets. That's what she'd said.

She would have to be satisfied with the memory of what they'd shared.

CHAPTER SIXTEEN

A lunchtime crowd filled The Brew Pub. Laughter, loud chatter, and the clatter of cutlery hitting plates filled the restaurant. Near the entrance, Diana craned her neck in search of her co-workers and spotted them when Jaclyn waved to get her attention.

Diana sidled past a female server nodding vigorously as the manager pointed to an empty booth that needed cleaning. Slipping past a boisterous table of women high-fiving each other, she dropped into the seat next to Jaclyn. "Sorry I'm late."

Trenton was back from his honeymoon, and her workload had picked up as he caught up with company business that occurred while he was gone.

"Don't worry about it." Corinne waved away the apology. She was a heavyset older woman, hair cut in a short natural like Diana's, except hers was almost completely gray. Having been at the company for years, she'd worked in multiple departments. She knew almost everyone and all the company gossip.

"I'm starving," Jaclyn said, trailing a finger down the menu. "I think I'm going to get the chicken sandwich. Anybody want to share an order of Wreck 'Em fries?"

"I'll split an order with you," Naylene said. The newest member of their group, she worked for two attorneys in the legal department. Diana saw her eating lunch by herself one day and invited her to join them.

"Perfect." Jaclyn closed the menu.

Naylene tucked a strand of straight strawberry blonde hair behind her ear. "And for lunch, I think I'll have…" She tapped her chin. "Heck, I'll have the chicken sandwich, too." She set down her menu.

Corinne leaned across the table. "Did you all hear—" She stared across the room, mouth falling open. "Look who just walked in," she said in a hushed voice.

Naylene's eyes brightened with interest, and both Diana and Jaclyn twisted around to follow the direction of their stares.

Xavier strolled over to the bar, elegant in a gray three-piece suit. Today he wore his hair pulled back from his face but hanging down his back.

"Lord have mercy, that man is beautiful," Corinne murmured.

Diana twisted around and dropped her unseeing gaze to the table. She gripped the menu as pain twisted in her chest. She hadn't seen Xavier since they returned from St. Louis over a week ago.

Corinne bit her bottom lip and slowly shook her head. "I have a weakness for men with dreadlocks, and here he is with all those dreadlocks, a tall drink of chocolate milk, and still single." She let out an exaggerated sigh.

"Aren't you old enough to be his mother?" Jaclyn asked.

Naylene covered her mouth and giggled.

"Old enough to be his big sister, thank you very much." Corrine straightened in the chair and glared at her. "Anyway, I may be older, but I'm not blind, sweetheart. Look at that man. You're so lucky you get to be on the top floor with him. Both of you."

"Hearing you talk about my boss like that is weird," Jaclyn muttered.

"How was your trip with him?" Corinne asked.

"Fine," Diana answered shortly.

"I would have sneaked into his hotel room," Naylene said.

"That would have been inappropriate," Diana said. She thought about what they'd done in her room and his. Inappropriate indeed. Deliciously so.

Naylene fanned her face. "The woman who gets him is a lucky woman."

"And he's such a good man," Corinne said, narrowing her eyes in such a way, Diana thought she might get up from the chair and jump Xavier's bones.

"What do you mean?" Naylene asked.

"Well, you know I've been here forever, since I'm old." She shot a dirty look at Jaclyn, who rolled her eyes. "Xavier is unique in his family. He actually left the family business and worked for a while in poorer communities around the world." She lowered her voice. "I was surprised when he started working for Johnson Enterprises, because rumor had it he thought capitalism was a bad thing. It's possible he's even ashamed of his wealth."

"Ashamed?" Naylene whispered. "What for?"

Corinne shrugged. "Who knows."

"Doesn't matter. He's rich and has a big heart. That's a good combination in a man." Naylene sighed.

"He's nice, but he's still got that Johnson blood," Corinne said.

"What do you mean by that?" Naylene asked.

"Honey, their father was hell on two legs, and Cyrus, the eldest, is just like their daddy. Isn't he?" She looked at Diana for confirmation.

Supposedly, the oldest had mellowed since he reconciled with his wife, but from what Diana could see it must all be on a personal level because he remained an indomitable force with only two goals: Make money. Make lots of money.

She nodded. "Cyrus is a tough one, but Xavier's nothing like him. I don't think," she added hastily, so as not to appear too familiar with him. She glanced at Jaclyn for confirmation.

"Not at all," Jaclyn agreed.

"Oh no?" One of Corinne's eyebrows lifted. "Then how did he end up in jail in Senegal?"

"What!" Naylene, Jaclyn, and Diana said at the same time.

"You never heard about that?" Corinne asked, excited to share juicy details about an incident they knew nothing about. She lowered her voice and leaned across the table. "Years ago he went to prison. Let's see, he started working here about two years ago, so I'd say maybe six…I don't know, seven years ago."

The waitress arrived, and Diana rushed through her order and waited impatiently as the others gave theirs. When the woman left, Diana opened her mouth to ask more questions, but Corinne interrupted her.

"There he goes," she said, eyes following Xavier.

Unable to resist, Diana twisted her head and watched him leave, a paper sack with his meal in hand. Broad-shouldered and wearing a commanding presence just as well as he wore the suit, he moved through the room nodding and smiling at staff and diners as he left. Each stride toward the door took him farther away from her, and Diana fisted a hand in her lap to fight back the longing to touch him and be touched by him again.

She wasn't supposed to feel like this. This achy, empty feeling in her chest was almost unbearable.

"So spill it." Naylene nudged Corinne's arm.

"I don't know *all* the details," Corinne said coyly, relishing her position as someone in the know. "I worked on a big project on the executive floor some years back and happened to overhear a conversation between Ivy and the oldest, Cyrus. Apparently, Xavier killed a man, and the villagers protested and he was arrested."

Jaclyn and Naylene gasped.

"Guess how he got away with it?" Corinne rubbed her thumb across her fingers to indicate *money*. "Paid people off. You know, the usual. When you're rich like that, you can do whatever you want."

Naylene's mouth fell open.

"I would have never guessed," Jaclyn said.

"Child, that's because they didn't want anyone to know. It was all very hush-hush, barely a blip in the news over here, but the incident was a big deal in Senegal."

They grew quiet when the waitress returned, delivered their drinks, and disappeared again.

"That doesn't sound like him," Diana said.

The three women looked at her.

Diana licked her lips nervously. "Does it sound like him to you?" she asked Jaclyn.

Jaclyn shook her head. "Actually, it doesn't."

"Are you saying I'm lying?" Corinne demanded.

"I'm saying maybe you misunderstood what you heard. He went to Senegal to help those people. Why would he murder someone?" She couldn't imagine Xavier committing such a violent crime, particularly in the country he felt such an affinity to. But she suspected something bad had happened over there by his reaction the night they talked at the pier. She cleared her throat. "You shouldn't spread rumors unless you know what you're saying is a fact."

Properly chastised, Corinne's mouth flattened. "That's what I heard." She shrugged.

They were silent for a while, conversations buzzing around them.

"Whatever happened, it's kinda sexy." Naylene bit her bottom lip.

"What is?" Jaclyn asked. She took a sip of water.

"You know, that he's so rich he could ignore the world's problems and enjoy his money and privilege, but...he chooses not to. He has a big heart."

"He sure does," Jaclyn agreed.

She'd been hired through a partnership Xavier established with a veteran's organization to source staff at Johnson Enterprises. Diana knew how appreciative Jaclyn was that he'd done something so many wouldn't do—look past her wheelchair to offer her a prestigious position as his executive assistant.

"You can think it's sexy all you want, but you'll never get a chance with a man like him," Corinne said.

"Not working in the legal department," Naylene grumbled. Her eyes brightened with mischief. "I could sneak up to the top floor, get into his office, lay spread eagle on the desk, and say, take me now!"

All four laughed.

"They don't let just anybody go up to the executive floor. Only staff on official company business are welcomed there," Corinne reminded her.

"I could pretend I'm working on a project with Jaclyn or Diana," Naylene said, one eyebrow arched and a sly grin on her lips.

"No way." Diana shook her head vigorously.

"Don't look at me, either," Jaclyn said.

Corinne laughed. "Child, please. Get that man out of your head right now. Having a fantasy is one thing, but be realistic. Men like Xavier Johnson don't end up with women like us."

Diana winced. Corinne had no idea how true those words were.

CHAPTER SEVENTEEN

Typical Monday. Everything that could go wrong went wrong.

First thing this morning, Xavier ended up stuck in traffic after an accident blocked the route on his way to work. For the second time in a week, he had Jaclyn reschedule a phone call with a Mexican brewery interested in a joint venture with Johnson Brewing Company. At this rate, the man would think he wasn't interested and was blowing him off.

After stepping foot in the office, he spent most of the morning on the phone, arguing with territory managers about margins.

Now this.

Xavier filed out of the small conference room after a videoconference meeting between him, three members of his team, and the managers at the Atlanta packaging plant. How none of them caught that JBC's labels for the new lager said Fall Moon beer instead of Full Moon beer blew his mind. He made it clear—succinctly and loudly—that he expected the labels redone and not one bottle to arrive late to a distributor. He didn't care if they had to work twenty-four hours every day to make it happen.

Xavier rolled his neck and took the elevator to the top floor. Truth be told, he hadn't been himself since St. Louis. He'd been cranky and short-tempered, and it seemed events at the company conspired to keep him in a perpetually foul mood.

The doors opened on the executive floor and Xavier saw Diana, Bryant, and the receptionist, Abigail, all crowded around Abigail's massive desk. Laughing and talking. Diana held a bouquet of red roses in a vase with three *Happy Birthday* balloons attached to it.

Stunned, he didn't move. Today was Diana's birthday?

Her smile—that radiant, vibrant smile—was directed at Bryant, who'd obviously brought her the gift. Abigail, wearing her headset, stood behind the desk, oohing and aahing over the bouquet.

Something inside Xavier snapped. He marched over to the group. "Do you have a reason to be on this floor?" he demanded of Bryant.

The happy faces disappeared. Abigail slowly lowered onto her chair and ducked her head, studying the calendar on her desk.

"I-I, ah…I came to see Diana," Bryant stuttered.

"These flowers don't look like official company business to me. Are you here on official company business?" Xavier asked.

Bryant swallowed. "No, sir."

"It's my fault. I gave him permission to come up." Diana's eyes darted between Xavier and Bryant.

Xavier glowered at her. "You gave him permission? Do you have some newfound authority I need to be made aware of?"

A spark of anger flared in her eyes. "No," she said between tight lips. "I—"

"The three of you need to wrap this up, and I want *you*"—he pointed at Diana—"in my office in five minutes." He marched off.

He was being an asshole, but he didn't care. She could giggle and flirt on her own damn time.

****

Diana walked into Xavier's offices like a prisoner on leaden feet. With a quick glance through the glass, she saw Jaclyn's closed office was empty. Standing outside his door, she steeled her nerves before knocking and entering. She found Xavier seated on the edge of the desk, arms crossed over his chest. Waiting.

His cold eyes landed on her. "Close the door," he said.

She hesitated but did as he asked.

"Come closer. I don't want to have to yell."

"I can hear you fine from here," Diana said.

"I said come closer."

She straightened her shoulders and took careful steps to get within feet of him.

"I sense an attitude," Xavier said.

"It's your imagination." She kept her face neutral and looked right at him.

"I don't think so."

She bit the inside of her lip to keep from saying something smart. "Do you want the truth?"

"Of course." He studied her with the same penetrating intensity as always, but this time it felt different. The heat of his ire practically seared her skin.

The words spilled from her lips in a rush. "You overreacted and chastised me in front of my co-workers. How dare you talk to me like—"

"How dare I?" He rose from the desk, and she took an involuntary step back. "Do you know who I am? This is my company. You had no business bringing another man...Bryant, up on this floor. Are you familiar with our company policy?" He snatched a sheet of paper from his desk and extended it to her.

Diana skimmed the page. It was printed from the employee manual, with the section concerning executive floor protocol highlighted in yellow.

"I am familiar with this company policy, but he only came as far as the reception desk. He was there for five minutes, to give me a birthday gift."

"Five minutes. Ten minutes. Company policy states that only employees conducting official business are allowed up on this floor. That includes Bryant. You know better. You breached company policy."

It hurt to hear him talk to her like that. After what they'd shared, he spoke to her as if she were any old employee—or worse, a stranger. As if she hadn't kissed him and licked his chest and he done the same to her. She wanted to hurt him, too. She wanted to strike back and make him feel a little of the pain tearing through her.

"Was having sex in St. Louis a breach of company policy, too?" she asked.

His eyes narrowed. "What did you say?"

"You heard me." She tilted up her chin.

"Are you threatening me?"

"Should I?" She would never turn him in to HR, but she thrilled at being able to unsettle him, even a little bit.

The silence in the room was deafening.

Xavier swallowed. "Are you seeing him?"

"That's none of your business." He didn't deserve an answer. Before today, he hadn't spoken a word to her since they returned from St. Louis. What she did and with whom was not his concern. She wouldn't give him the satisfaction of knowing that Bryant was only a friend.

"Are you seeing him?"

"What do you care? I can see whoever I want."

He came closer. "Are you seeing him!"

"I don't belong to you!" Diana yelled.

"Yes, you do!" he ground out, his voice raw.

Her eyes widened. He was breathing hard and so was she.

"No, I don't," Diana said in a quieter voice.

She heard the labored way he sucked air into his lungs and saw the tension in his body as he restrained himself, fisting his hands at his sides. "No, you don't." His mouth transformed into a bitter twist.

"Are we done?" Diana asked.

He came closer, stepping deep into her personal space, but she stayed put.

"I don't want to have to call you into my office for your conduct again. Make sure you do what you're told. Is that clear?"

"Yes, sir," she answered in a tart, flippant tone.

Half a second before he reached for her, the low growl and flash in his eyes issued a warning. Her breath quickened when he grabbed her by the neck and dragged her against his chest.

His mouth came down in an angry kiss that sent aching need and blinding passion coursing through her veins. Instead of pushing him away, Diana shuddered and groaned, clutching onto his vest and kissing him back.

He pushed her backwards and seconds later she was on her stomach, bent over his desk. The drag of a zipper sounded in the room. She knew she should stop him—push him away for the way he'd ignored her since their return. Yet she couldn't summon the strength, even as he forced her legs wide and yanked her dress up past her hips.

She wanted it. She positioned herself to take him.

Xavier pushed aside her panties and cupped her wet mound. His touch was possessive, as if to prove she did belong to him.

Using a quick thrust, he replaced his hand with his thick shaft. Diana cried out as he shoved his length deep in her body. To stem the sounds of ecstasy, she curled her fingers atop the cool wooden desk and bit down on her lip. Each thrust of his hips had her sinking her teeth into her own flesh until the faint metallic taste of blood touched the tip of her tongue.

Spreading her fingers, she pushed back and contracted her muscles. He groaned, temporarily losing his rhythm and then increasing the speed of his pumping hips.

She caught the dim reflection of them in the window. She, bent over the desk. Xavier's hands on her hips and head bent in concentration as he sexed her within an inch of her life. The sight of them together in such a wanton position, in his office, in the middle of the day, took her to the brink. Two hard slaps on her ass from his hand sent her over the edge.

She let out an involuntary cry, free-falling into a stomach-clenching climax.

Behind her, Xavier spasmed, emptying into the condom he'd had the prudence to put on. At least one of them was thinking clearly.

He eased out of her and went into the adjoining bathroom. Diana took the short period apart to stand on shaky legs and straighten her dress. Her cheeks burned. The scent of him was in her clothes. Everyone would know.

"Diana, I don't know what to say. I didn't...that's not why I called you back here." He spoke behind her. His voice sounded wooden and emotionless.

She turned to face him. "No, you called me back here to chastise me."

"This shouldn't have happened. I lost control. I can't..." He blew a puff of frustrated air through his mouth and ran his hands down his face. "I don't know what the hell is happening to me," he muttered.

"While you figure it out, I'll go back to work. If you'll excuse me..." She rushed toward the door, escaping before he could stop her.

"Diana, wait!"

They ran into Jaclyn in the hall, entering her own office with a stack of papers on her lap. His assistant looked from one to the other. Had she heard them? Diana's stomach tangled into a big knot.

Jaclyn cleared her throat, averted her eyes, and scooted into her office.

She knew. Diana wanted to die.

"Diana." His voice sounded grave, and when she turned to him the expression on his face was equally somber as his voice.

"I'm not a whore, Xavier," she whispered, shaking. "I don't appreciate you treating me like one." She hurried away from him.

****

Xavier sank into his chair, guilt the weight of a ton of stone lying heavy in his gut. Watching Diana run away left him feeling deflated, like a flattened tire.

Twenty-four hours. That's all she'd needed from him, yet he couldn't curtail his need for her and had attacked her like a wild savage, hoping to brand her so she wouldn't have need for another man.

Xavier closed his eyes and rested the back of his head against the chair. She wasn't his, but he wanted her to be.

He swiveled in the chair and tapped his computer keyboard. Scrolling through the office directory, he found the number he needed. He hesitated, thinking. This was a mistake. He knew it, but felt compelled to proceed.

Before he could change his mind, he picked up the phone and dialed human resources.

CHAPTER EIGHTEEN

Wednesday after lunch, Xavier stepped off the elevator and ran into Gavin. "Can I talk to you?" his brother asked.

"Sure. I need to talk to you, too."

The walk back to his office was quiet. When the door closed behind them, Gavin started. "I had an interesting conversation with one of my managers, and I'm sure there must be some misunderstanding. She told me you transferred Bryant Wheeler to Portland." He appeared calm, but crossed his arms over his chest—which meant he definitely was not calm.

Xavier sighed. "I meant to tell you about the transfer—"

"You meant to tell me?" Gavin repeated in disbelief. "When? When exactly did you intend to tell me you've transferred a member of *my* staff to another state? Don't you think we should have had that conversation before you started the ball rolling?"

"Calm down, Gavin."

"Nah, I won't calm down. You moved one of my employees from my department without consulting me."

"There wasn't time."

"What was the rush?"

"I made the decision because I thought he could do a good job in the Portland facility. End of story."

Gavin cocked his head in disbelief. "And you didn't think you could discuss your idea with me?"

"I should have. It was an oversight."

Gavin chuckled. "What is going on with you? That's not an oversight, Xavier. That's blatant disrespect."

"There was nothing disrespectful in my decision, and I planned to tell you. A position opened up—"

"What position and when?"

At the interruption, Xavier counted to three and calmed down. It was a position he'd created himself. "Quality assurance technician, two days ago," he said firmly.

"There may be someone more qualified."

"He's perfect for the job. He's interested and able to move right away because he has no ties to Seattle."

"You have this all figured out, don't you?" Gavin glared at him. "But the move to Portland doesn't make sense. You barely know Bryant and my manager said you never consulted her about his qualifications."

"I didn't need to. I touched base with HR and got a good grasp of his skillsets and determined they were what we need in the role." If he'd gotten Gavin involved, he would have delayed getting Bryant out of there quickly, if at all.

"This is some bullshit, Xavier, and I don't appreciate you undermining my authority."

"You're blowing the transfer out of proportion."

"How would you feel if I yanked someone from your staff and transferred them to another department? Or better yet, how about I go over your head and consult with Cyrus, make a decision, and exclude you from the decision-making process?"

Xavier's mouth tightened.

"Yeah, you wouldn't like that, would you? Still jealous of your big brother and his relationship with our father?" Gavin said.

"You're a fine one to talk."

"I've worked through my shit. How about you?"

"I don't have any shit to work through."

"Oh, really? So you no longer think you're better than the rest of us?"

He'd heard that accusation before. "I never thought I was better than anybody."

He volunteered all those years because he wanted to. The work gave him a sense of accomplishment, made him feel as if he was leaving his mark on the world in a positive way. "The good one" was not a term he called himself, but he was expected to live up to it.

"With the move you pulled, you sure proved you aren't, and frankly, you never were. No matter how much you try to run from it, you're like the rest of us. Embrace who you are. You come from a life of privilege, went to the same private schools, and have the same blood running through your veins."

Xavier chuckled to himself. "I'm sick and tired of you, Cyrus, and everybody else who insists on telling me what I feel or how I think. For the record, I'm proud of the work I've done. Unlike you, who spent your time partying around the world and chasing ass, I spent my time helping people."

Gavin nodded slowly. "True, you have plenty to be proud of, except for that incident in Senegal you don't like to talk about. Am I right? Because let's be honest, you're the only one of us who ended up with a criminal record in a foreign prison."

Xavier quietly seethed. "You know why that happened," he said in a low tone.

"Yeah. You messed up. Overstepped your bounds there, too."

Their gazes clashed, and neither would look away.

"Run your department any way you want, but the next time you want to make a decision in *my* department, talk to me first." Gavin stalked toward the door.

Anger pulsed inside of Xavier. "I am the goddamn COO of this company. I don't make decisions by consensus. That's not my role."

Gavin turned slowly. His light brown eyes, flashed in anger. "No, your role is to manage the operations of this company." He jabbed a finger at him. "You don't make decisions in my department without consulting me first. Get your ego out of the way."

"I don't have a problem with my ego," Xavier said between gritted teeth.

"You've always had an ego problem, but you wouldn't admit it. We all have ego. Hell, it's an inherited trait. The thing is your ego is built around the fact that you want to be some kind of savior, and you make your decisions accordingly. Even with this Morse Brewing deal—it's a cut-and-dried situation. If it's a good financial decision, we move forward, if not, we pull back. But you want to argue about whether or not we can save the employees."

"We can do both."

"How much more time are we going to waste trying to work out a solution that includes saving the workforce? Because I know that's what you're doing. Yet a position opens up one day, and you've already filled it with an employee you hardly know anything about. I don't know what's gotten into you, what would prompt you to—" He frowned. "Wait a minute. You asked me about Bryant at the wedding, when he was sitting with Diana, and according to office gossip, she and he..." His eyebrows lifted as a thought came to him.

Deafening silence descended on the room.

"Don't tell me this is about Diana," Gavin said, narrowing his eyes on Xavier. "Are you sleeping with her?"

Silence.

"Are you insane? She's a subordinate. You're opening a can of worms, and you better be careful around Cyrus, because if he finds out you're sleeping with her —"

"I've got it under control."

"I don't think you do. Not when you're letting what you feel for this woman affect your decision-making."

"This conversation is over. Should I have gotten in touch with you first, yes. But I made my decision, and it's the right one for the company. Bryant will be moving to Portland next week. A relocation coordinator has already been in touch with him to help him find temporary housing and ensure a smooth transition." Xavier walked around his desk. "Now if you'll excuse me, I have work to do." He sat down.

Gavin let out a long whistle. "Moving next week. You didn't waste any time. And your decision didn't have anything to do with Diana? Yeah, right. Such good behavior coming from a man who prides himself on always doing the right thing." Gavin walked over and splayed his hands on the desk. "You may hold a higher position, but our ownership interest is the same in this company. Don't forget that. Next time you get a bright idea, run it by me first. Otherwise we're going to have major problems."

Gavin pushed away and strolled toward the door.

When he was gone, Xavier grabbed his Mont Blanc pen and tossed it against the bookcase. It landed with a soft thud on the carpet.

CHAPTER NINETEEN

"Come on, give me a few more!"

The voice of the trainer, a baldheaded former heavyweight boxer named Dondre, echoed in Xavier's home gym. He stood with his legs braced and shoulder-width apart, hands holding a professional grade punching bag in place.

Teeth gritted, Xavier's gloved fists slammed into the heavy bag. Sweat glistened on his naked chest and shoulders, dripping down the sides of his face. He kept pounding relentlessly. His fists connected with lethal force each time.

"Thirty more seconds," the trainer said.

Xavier landed blow after blow after blow. His hair, styled in a folded over ponytail to keep the dreadlocks off his neck, bounced when each punch landed.

"Ten seconds."

His biceps and triceps burned from the physical exertion.

"Nine, eight, seven…"

Xavier punched faster.

"Two…one. Great job."

Xavier fired off a few more blows in rapid succession and then stepped away from the bag. Chest heaving as air gushed from his lungs like a geyser, he rested his gloved hands on his knees and closed his eyes. The early morning workout was just what he'd needed.

He straightened and opened his eyes.

Dondre grinned. "Something tells me you really, really needed that."

Resting his hands on his hips, Xavier let his head fall back and released a heavy breath. "More than you know." He hadn't meditated in over a week. Unleashing vicious blows to the punching bag seemed the only safe way to expend the pent-up frustration that plagued him.

"Don't tell me you're getting soft now that you're a corporate man."

"Either that or I'm getting old."

Dondre starting unlacing Xavier's gloves. "How old are you? Thirty-six, right?"

"Almost."

"I'm older, so spare me the I'm-getting-old complaint. You work too much. That's the real problem."

Xavier lifted his lukewarm bottle of water from the floor and chugged a mouthful. He swiped the back of his hand across his mouth. "I wish it were work," he said.

He couldn't stop thinking about his volatile reaction to seeing Diana and Bryant together. What had he, Xavier, been to her? A sexual experiment? A stud to get back into the groove until she moved on to a relationship with another man?

Dondre tossed him a towel and Xavier wiped the sweat from his face. "That only leaves one other thing—woman problems."

"Is there any other kind?"

Dondre let out a bark of laughter. "It always comes back to the fairer sex. They rule the world."

"Tell me about it. If they ever figure that out, we'll really be in trouble."

Dondre chuckled again, and they left the gym. Xavier escorted him through the house, sneakers squeaking on the marble floors.

"Like what you've done to the place." Dondre looked up at the exposed beams in the eighteen-foot ceilings.

"Thanks."

The renovations had created a harmonious blend of modern and rustic décor at the multi-acre property. His four-bedroom home—formerly five bedrooms before he converted one of them into a meditation room—with a three-car garage was modest compared to the large estates his mother and siblings owned. The tranquility of the location had prompted him to buy it. The property had plenty of greenspace and a view of Elliott Bay. Because of its size, he didn't need a full staff. A house manager and contracted maid service sufficed.

Dondre walked through the front door. "You know where to find me when you're ready for a real workout again."

"See you later, old man," Xavier said with a laugh.

Dondre sent a backward wave as he walked to his car.

Xavier showered and donned a black Ozwald Boateng suit with a black tie. He secured his hair in the back so that it was pulled away from his face and allowed to flow down his back.

Satisfied with his appearance, he retrieved his briefcase and left the bedroom. He walked through the house to the huge kitchen, sleekly designed with gray cabinets, quartz countertops, and Viking appliances which he seldom touched since cooking was not his strength. The same blend of modern and rustic carried over into this room with wooden floors that matched the exposed beams overhead.

He set his briefcase on one of the chairs in the breakfast nook.

"Good morning, sir." Thomas, the house manager stood at the long island slicing fruit.

He lived on the property in a one-bedroom guesthouse. Thirty years older than Xavier, his head was covered in short-cropped, salt and pepper curls. Xavier didn't require he wear a uniform, but Thomas was old school and preferred to do so. It consisted of a loose-fitting gray top and darker pants.

"Good morning. How's Lindsay?" Xavier picked up the vitamins from the quartz countertop and swallowed them with a glass of lukewarm water.

Thomas's brown face broke into a smile. "Excellent. Recovering nicely and not looking forward to going back to school in a few days, I'm afraid." His granddaughter had her tonsils taken out. "She received the gifts you sent. Thank you very much."

"Happy to do it." Xavier had sent enough flowers, balloons, and stuffed animals to fill the little girl's room.

Thomas dumped the fruit into a blender, along with hempseeds, spinach, and almond milk, and the sound of the blender's motor filled the air.

Xavier studied the grounds outside the window, and when Thomas cut off the blender, he said, "Tell the landscapers to cut back the shrubs from the stone pathway leading away from the house. I want a clear path to the koi pond."

"Already ahead of you, sir. I spoke to them about it yesterday."

"Are they delivering the fish today?"

"Yes, sir. They'll be here at eleven." Thomas poured the smoothie into a travel cup.

Xavier took it. "What would I do without you, Thomas?"

"I hope you never have to find out, sir," Thomas said, a twinkle in his eye.

Chuckling, Xavier retrieved his briefcase and exited through the front door, where Cliff, his driver, waited next to the SUV.

Xavier greeted him with a nod. "Cliff."

"Good morning."

He settled into the backseat and sipped the smoothie before dialing Gavin's number. Time to make amends.

Gavin answered. "What do you want, Xavier?"

Obviously, he wasn't going to make this easy for him. "You always were a damn brat, you know that?"

"You called to insult me?"

"No." Sighing, Xavier rubbed a hand across his forehead. "About that situation with Bryant, it shouldn't have happened and won't happen again. I was wrong."

There was a moment of silence. Then finally, Gavin said, "I appreciate you calling."

"So we're good?"

"Yeah." Gavin cleared his throat. "What's the deal with you and Diana?"

"I'm still figuring it out. I need to figure it out before my head explodes."

"Something tells me you've already made a decision," Gavin said.

Xavier watched the traffic go by. "You might be right," he conceded. He'd never been so obsessed with a woman before, and he couldn't continue like this.

"So what's the plan?" Gavin asked.

"No other woman will do, so I'm going to make her mine."

****

Diana sat on the sofa in her bathrobe, feet propped up on the coffee table. In the middle of a *Law & Order* marathon, the doorbell rang. She ignored it and continued watching the show. Seconds later, the bell rang again, more insistently this time. She continued to ignore it. No one knew she was home, so they could go away with whatever they were selling.

A loud knock sounded on the door. Angry at their persistence, she jumped up from the sofa and shuffled to the front door. Through the peephole, Xavier's dark eyes stared back at her.

She tugged the robe tighter, as if it could protect her from the heat of his stare.

"What do you want, Xavier?"

"I'm here because I'm concerned about you."

"There's nothing to be concerned about. I'm fine." She rested her head on the door.

"Open the door. Please."

Already her hand was reaching for the lock, and she opened the door.

"Are you all right? Trenton told me you took a sick day."

"I'm fine. I had a dentist appointment this morning, but I took the entire day off."

"Are you alone?"

For a fleeting second, she thought about lying. "Yes," she answered truthfully.

"Can I come in?"

"Why?"

"We need to talk."

"Whatever you have to say can be said right there."

"Let me in, Diana."

Having him use that tone of voice should have upset her, but instead it sent a thrill of excitement rippling down her spine. Diana eased the door open and he walked in.

She leaned on the closed door.

"We need to talk about Bryant."

"You got rid of him."

When Bryant came to her and explained he'd be moving to Portland, she hadn't mustered even a smidgen of disappointment. They weren't in a relationship, and they never would be. Because all she thought about was Xavier.

"He received a transfer to Portland," Xavier said.

"Like I said, you got rid of him."

His mouth firmed. "Yes, I got rid of him. He was in my way." He came closer and braced his hands on either side of her.

"So now what? You think you can use me whenever you feel like?" she whispered.

"Absolutely not."

"I don't like you very much right now."

He leaned in close. "Why not?" The twin mahogany pools of his eyes contemplated her appearance, dragging over the blue terrycloth robe. "Because you don't like it when I touch you?" He brushed his nose along her cheek.

"You yelled at me and treated me like I was…" Her throat tightened. "You didn't even say happy birthday. Slam, bam, thank you, ma'am."

"I'm sorry."

He touched her cheek and she twisted away her face.

"This entire situation is complicated enough for me, without you making it harder."

"Why is it so hard?"

"Because…" she whispered, tightening her hands into fists at her sides, "All I do is think about you."

"All I do is think about you, too. So what should we do about that?" He trailed a finger down her cheek. His mouth followed. "What do you think?"

Helplessly, she leaned into him. "This is insane. We were supposed to be done after Missouri," she whispered.

"We were just getting started in Missouri."

He kissed her and she kissed him back, opening her mouth for the invasion of his tongue. She could never get enough of this man. Never, ever.

He cupped her face in his hands. "I've spent half my life trying to be different from my father and brother. The opposite of arrogant, pushy, and difficult. But I've come to accept that I have some of that in me, and that sometimes, you have to be arrogant, pushy, and difficult to get what you want. And you, Diana, are what I want. All of you. All the time. Twenty-four hours was not nearly enough."

Whimpering, Diana wrapped her arms around his neck and pressed her body into his. She gripped a handful of his hair and opened her mouth for a thorough kiss. Darts of pleasure stuck her skin everywhere she came into contact with him.

With his arm around her waist, Xavier guided Diana into the living room onto the sofa and pulled her on top of him so that she straddled his legs.

"Tell me you're mine," he whispered into her neck. "Tell me no other man gets to touch you but me."

Diana cupped his face in her hands. "No one. I don't want anyone else but you," she breathed.

He pushed the robe from her shoulders and sucked her breasts through the lace cups of her black bra. His impatience stirred heat in her loins and spurred her on with the need to give him pleasure.

She lowered to her knees and gave him a blow job, servicing him until he spilled his seed on her tongue with a helpless grunt of surrender. Then she straddled his thighs, and he took her to ecstasy with lovemaking so good she couldn't feel her legs afterward.

There was no point in running from this heat. This type of fire couldn't be easily quenched.

Xavier made her feel like no other man before him.

Beautiful. Sexy. Alive.

CHAPTER TWENTY

Diana came back into her bedroom to find Xavier sitting up against the headboard, leafing through the book *10 O-inducing Positions for Plus-Size Women.*

"Where did you get that?" she asked, eyes wide.

"You left it on the nightstand," he said.

"Give me that!" She lunged for the book.

Xavier held it out of reach. "Well, well, well, interesting reading."

"Give it to me," she said.

"Is that what they tell you to say?" he teased. "It's a little demanding, but I can work with it."

"Ha. Ha." She climbed under the sheets and tugged the robe tighter around her body.

Chuckling, he flipped a page. "Hmm. We did that in the office the other day," he murmured. The image showed a woman bent over a table with a man behind her.

"You're terrible, you know that?" Diana settled on her side, propped up by the pillows.

"Huh. This looks interesting." Xavier showed her the diagram of a woman on her side, her partner penetrating her from behind and his hands cupping her breasts. "We haven't tried that position yet."

"We should try that next," she said quietly, biting her lip.

"I agree."

Xavier set aside the book and helped Diana out of the robe. Then he pulled her into his arms. She let out a contented moan as he rubbed her back and bottom and thighs. He enjoyed touching her. She was so soft everywhere.

"Why didn't you tell me it was your birthday the other day?"

She shrugged. "It never came up."

"We have to do something. I can't let Bryant upstage me."

"Isn't it enough you got rid of him?"

Xavier growled. "Were you seeing him?"

"No. He was interested, but we were only friends."

"I'm glad to hear it, but he still had to go."

Her lips curved against his skin. He liked making her smile. He wanted to make her smile, laugh, and weep with joy.

"How about dinner and a show?"

"I like that idea."

"We could fly down to Vegas."

Her head popped up. "Are you serious? I thought you meant dinner and a show here."

"We could do that, but you deserve something special for your thirty-fifth birthday."

She kissed him. "Dinner, a show, and birthday sex sounds good," she said softly.

"Excellent idea!"

Giggling, she nestled her head in the crook of his neck and shoulder, lying half on top of him. "I like being able to talk to you about sex. After getting shut down for years, it's so...refreshing."

"You can talk to me about anything, Diana. Always." He kissed her forehead.

She was quiet for a while. Then she said, "Can I ask you a question?"

"I said you can talk to me about anything. I meant it."

She still hesitated. Finally, she tilted her head to look at his face. "What happened in Senegal?"

He tensed.

"Maybe I shouldn't have asked," she murmured.

"No, I said anything and I meant anything, but Senegal is a topic I generally don't talk about."

"Why?" she asked quietly.

"Because my time there ended disastrously," he said shortly.

Diana lifted onto an elbow to look at him. "The night we ate at the pier, I could tell something had happened."

Xavier scrubbed his fingers through his locs. Senegal was the biggest failure of his life. "People got hurt." He faced her. "And it was my fault."

"I doubt that."

"Maybe not entirely my fault, but I was partly to blame." He stared up at the ceiling. "A Saudi investment company was trying to take over land owned by local farmers, for rice production. It's happening in other West African countries—Mali, Nigeria. What they do is take the most productive farmland and export the rice to the Kingdom."

"What about the local farmers?" Diana asked.

"They're run off and left with no way to make a living." He still grew furious when he considered how behind-closed-door deals between greedy government officials and foreign corporations could so negatively affect the well-being of thousands—millions of people. "To slow the land grab, I brokered a deal between one rural community and myself and other financial backers. Using a third party, we'd loan them the money at a low interest rate to get the technology they needed to fight pest infestation and increase production. A few days before they were to sign the agreement in a local ceremony, the chief elder went missing. His body turned up a few days later. They'd shot him in the back of the head."

Diana gasped and covered her mouth. "Do you know who did it?"

He shrugged. "No way to know for sure. Could have been someone in the government, someone with the corporation, or even a local who thought we were wrong for stopping progress. All I know is, a man was killed because I pushed for change."

"Xavier, you can't blame yourself. You were doing the right thing to help those people."

"Maybe at first, but I didn't do the right thing when I went down to the government office." He ran a hand down his face. His blood had been boiling that day. "Maybe I took it too personally because…because that's *my* family's home. My people come from there. I rounded up a group of men and we marched down to the agriculture office. I told myself we were going to talk to them, but deep down I knew that wasn't our intention. We trashed the place. Broken glass, overturned desks, the works. The police attacked one of my friends—the young man whose father had been killed—with a club, and I defended him. I threw the police officer off of him. More came at me, and I fought them. It was a mess."

"That's how you ended up in jail."

"Pretty much. Me and a group of twenty-two men were arrested for assault and vandalism. They tossed us all in jail. I was banned from the country for inciting a riot."

A bitter pill to swallow and a crushing blow—to be banned from the country where he could trace his roots. A place where he'd felt at home. He still recalled how the hairs rose on his arms as he stepped off the plane that first day. As if the ghosts of his ancestors had reached out and dragged their fingers along his arms.

"My family's lawyers worked with lawyers in-country to get me out, but I couldn't leave those men behind. I told the lawyers I wouldn't leave unless they could negotiate their release, too. It took a while, but all the fines were paid and we all got out."

"Of course, you'd have to pay bribes." Diana shook her head. "The corruption in those countries…"

Xavier snorted. "Corruption is not unique to those countries. We have state governments that allow poisonous water to flow into the homes of its residents and a privatized prison system where judges take bribes to shuffle our citizens into cells for profit. I could go on and on with more examples. Are we really any different? Wherever there are human beings, there's corruption."

"I never thought of it that way," Diana said.

"My only regret is that once I was released, I had to leave the country right away. I got to fly out on a private jet, but the men I left behind had to live there. I felt like I'd left my people behind.

Abandoned them. I'm sure there were repercussions." The guilt and regret still ate at him.

"Do you know what happened to the land purchase?"

"My contacts said it went through. A man was dead, and those people still lost their land."

Diana twirled one of his locks around her finger. "Why do you care so much?" she asked.

His gaze drifted to her. "My father used to say that we're in a unique position to leave the world in a better state than we found it, and it's our moral duty to do so. My father was consumed with success and making money, but it was one of the few things we actually agreed on."

She looked at him, as if seeing him for the first time. "You're a special man, Xavier."

"There's nothing special about me."

"You're wrong. You're very special. You're one of a kind."

CHAPTER TWENTY-ONE

"You have to get up. You've got to go," Diana said.

Despite her admonitions, she didn't want Xavier to leave for lunch at his mother's. In the past few weeks, every time they separated, she felt as if a piece of her, some organ that was essential to survival, left her body.

Having just come in from the kitchen, she strolled across the bedroom floor in his pajama top and climbed into bed with him. She unbuttoned the top and pressed her bare breasts to his back. Throwing an arm across his waist and a leg over hip, she said, "Get up."

He hooked his hand behind her knee and dragged her tighter against his body. "I don't want to. Not with those luscious breasts pressing into my back. I'm never moving."

Laughing, Diana brushed his hair back from his neck so she could rest her cheek on his, feeling the morning scruff against her skin. She smoothed a hand up and down his chest, over the sprinkling of hairs on his six-pack abs, and back up again to his muscular pecs.

She'd been up with him since dawn, when they went for a walk around the property. She loved his home. It was the place she felt most at peace—this arboreal escape with fresh breezes and acres of greenery. The rustic splendor of the property gave the sense of being in a remote, far away locale, when in actuality it was minutes from the city.

An hour ago they'd climbed back into bed to make love. With her son at her parents' house in California, she'd spent every night this week at Xavier's and even joined him in his evening meditation, a relaxing ritual she planned to continue when she resumed sleeping at her place.

They still hadn't gone public with their relationship. They arrived separately to work each day, an arrangement she insisted on, concerned about what people would say if they saw them coming in together.

"Did I hurt you last night?" He rubbed a thumb over her red wrist.

"No. I just bruise easily."

"If I ever—"

"I'm fine. I promise."

He turned onto his back and looked at her. "A couple of months ago you had bruises on your wrist. Was that from—"

"No," she said quickly. "I wasn't seeing anyone. You're the first lover I've had since my divorce."

"So what happened?"

"My ex was being a jerk." She rolled her eyes.

Xavier went still. "What did he do?"

"He grabbed me."

"Grabbed you?" His brow furrowed. "Does he do that often?"

"No. He can be a bully, but he knows better."

His face hardened. "He better."

She stroked his face. "Why? What do you plan to do?"

"Beat his ass."

"I appreciate your concern, but I promise, that's not necessary. I can handle Rodrick." Xavier was silent as she climbed on top of him, straddling his hips. "I'm going to beat your ass if you don't hurry up and get dressed."

"That's not possible, sweetheart."

"Oh yeah?"

"Yeah."

She grasped his wrists and held them against the pillow over his head. "What do you have to say for yourself now?"

A slow, sexy movement of his lips made her want to kiss him.

With what seemed like minimal effort, he flipped her onto her back and pinned her arms above her head with one hand.

"Really? You thought you could contain me?" he asked. His hair tumbled over one shoulder in a curtain of dark rope.

She laughed. "I could. If I were stronger."

"That makes no sense. That's like saying I could fly if I had wings."

Her eyes widened in mock anger. "No, it's not."

"Yeah, it is. But I'll let it pass." His eyes dropped to the open shirt that left her breasts exposed. "I see what you're doing—distracting me…" He kissed the valley between her breasts and licked the tip of the right one. She spread her legs so he could press comfortably against her wet mound.

Diana whimpered. "We don't have time for this."

His mouth had moved to the underside of her breast, his moist kisses and the new growth of hair on his face aroused her further. "Then why'd you open your legs?"

Diana gasped, arching her back as he sucked her breast. "I can't help it," she moaned.

She wanted him all the time. He barely touched her and her skin set aflame with uncontrollable lust. He'd unleashed a greedy, insatiable monster in her that never seemed to get enough.

Xavier still held her hands above her head, so she was completely at the mercy of his mouth and grinding hips.

"That means you don't want me to stop." He kissed his way up to her neck, and Diana arched her back even farther, tilting back her head and elongating her neck for his mouth. "This is my bed, and I'll tell you when it's time to go," he said. "Understand?"

"Yes." Her voice shook, her body growing wetter at the guttural steel in his voice. She loved it when he talked to her like that.

"Who's in charge?"

"You are," she breathed.

He lifted an ankle onto his shoulder and notched his body into hers.

He held her pinned down as he kissed her, hips rolling on top of hers. The slow, even grind of his pelvis against her clit inflamed the swollen flesh. Their lovemaking was slow and measured, but no less explosive. When she came, her entire body quivered beneath him. Groaning above her, Xavier took deep, heaving breaths and thrust faster, until he emptied inside her.

Afterward, they lay on their backs until their lungs could function at normal capacity.

"Now I'm definitely going to be late. I'm telling my mother it's your fault."

Diana giggled. "Don't you dare."

He rolled to face her. "Come with me." He ran a caressing hand over her short hair.

"It's not a good idea."

"Why not?"

Her stomach tensed. "I'm not ready. You know that."

"When will you be ready?" Amusement was long gone from his eyes.

Diana felt herself falling faster off her high. She avoided his gaze, but he brought a hand under her chin and tilted up her face, forcing her to look him in the eye.

"When will you be ready?" he asked again, this time a little bit of irritation in his voice.

She understood his displeasure, but she had her doubts. Could he change? Could this gentle but firm prince turn into an ogre? It wasn't fair to compare him to her past relationship, but Xavier was moving fast, and Rodrick had moved fast, too.

"I can't right now," Diana said. She wanted to enjoy the newness of their relationship a little longer.

He rolled away and sat up with his back to her.

"We talked about this," she reminded him. "My life is complicated."

"We can work through any complication."

"It's not that easy, Xavier. I need you to be patient a little bit longer."

He gave a short laugh. "For a long time I didn't make any of my relationships public, and here I am in the same situation. Now I know how those women felt." He rose from the bed, exposing his naked body—the taut glutes, the muscular back.

"I want to," she said, watching him head toward the closet.

He stopped at the door. "Then do it. Come with me."

Diana shook her head.

"How long do you want to hide our relationship? For the next two years? The next three?"

"I don't want to argue with you."

"Yeah." He laughed sarcastically and walked into the closet.

Diana jumped up and followed him. "You know as well as I do that it's not simply lunch. It's a big step." When he remained silent, she asked, "Won't Trenton be there?"

"He may or may not be, depending on what he and his new wife are doing. They may be holed up in their condo, for all I know."

Xavier used the smaller of the two closets in the bedroom. His was a long, rectangular room made of cedar, with clothes and shoes filling almost every shelf and hanger. He went to the island in the middle of the floor and opened a drawer. He pulled out a leather dreadlocks cuff and secured his hair with it.

"What do you expect?" she asked.

"I expect you to eat lunch with us and laugh at my jokes like you always do."

"Xavier, you know my situation."

"Actually, I don't know your situation, Diana. Why don't you tell me all about it?"

"I have a kid. You seem to want to get serious, and I...I have to think about him and his welfare in everything I do."

"You expect me to believe this is about Andre? Try again. Your son has nothing to do with you coming to my mother's luncheon," he said dismissively. He tugged on boxer briefs and a pair of jeans.

"So you want me to jump feet-first into this commitment thing?"

"Commitment thing?" he repeated with disgust. "I don't know what a commitment thing is, but I can tell you that I'm committed to you. To us. You're clearly not. We're just having a good time."

"You think you know me so well."

"I know you very well, and you're lying." He slammed the drawer and opened another one.

"What the hell do you want from me, Xavier?"

"I want you to be honest. For once, Diana."

She shriveled inside at the harsh tone. Since they'd become a couple, he'd never spoken to her in anger before. Annoyed, yes. Angry, no.

"Be honest about the way you feel, because I'm not your ex, and this nonsense about your son is nothing but an excuse." He yanked a shirt from the drawer—a white cotton shirt with a dashiki design around the neckline, and pulled it over his head.

"Fine! You want honesty, here it is. I don't want to fail again."

He stopped moving. Waited. Focused on her.

Suddenly feeling exposed, Diana pulled the pajama top closed and crossed her arms defensively over her stomach. "I stayed...in a sexless, loveless marriage because I didn't want to fail. I couldn't tell anyone my husband wouldn't touch me. I tried so hard to make him want me. I rented porn, which he hated. I bought wigs and sexy lingerie, and he called me a whore." Her voice trembled at the memories of the volatile arguments and his constant rejection. "Nothing worked. The harder I tried, the more disgusted he became."

Diana stared down at the floor.

"I told myself, sure, he wouldn't touch me, but I should be happy he wasn't cheating on me the way my father cheated on my mother. He loved me and we had a comfortable life. That should be enough, right? Except it wasn't." She looked at Xavier again. "I wanted more. I wanted to wake up with my husband's arms around me. I wanted him to hold and kiss me. I wanted him to make love to me, and he couldn't do any of those things.

"After he moved into our spare bedroom, I finally accepted he never would do any of those things and maybe I wasn't being petty or selfish. Sex *is* an important aspect of a relationship. At least…it's important to me. Being with someone for whom it wasn't important, made us incompatible and put a strain on our marriage. I didn't want to leave Rodrick. I wanted to resolve our issues, but sleeping in separate bedrooms meant there was no hope for us. I had a roommate, when what I really wanted was a husband. After I left him, Rodrick changed for the worst. He became angrier and more bitter—downright resentful of me moving on. That's when our disagreements flared up into full-blown verbal abuse."

"Did you consider therapy?"

She scoffed at the question. "He wouldn't go to therapy. To this day, I don't know what's wrong with him. I have my suspicions, but I can't say for sure. For the longest time I thought it was me. I ended up hiding my true self. My friends, my son, my job became my focus.

"During our marriage, he accused me of sleeping with other men, which was absolutely untrue. I won't lie and say I wasn't tempted—and believe me, I felt guilty about it—but I never cheated on my husband. To put his mind at ease, I went to work for him for a while, became his assistant, helped him with the real estate business. He was my focus. I gave and I gave. Patience, attention, money to help his business—everything I could, but I couldn't change our situation. It became…untenable. I was losing myself. My younger, wiser cousin Camille convinced me to quit and find a different job. Working with other people gradually gave me my confidence back. But there are times when I still feel like a failure. There must have been something more I could do."

"You're not a failure. You couldn't change him anymore than he could change you. Like you said, you were incompatible. You and I, on the other hand, are *very* compatible."

Diana's cheeks heated, and Xavier took her hands in his and rubbed his thumbs across her knuckles.

"You should come to lunch with me. My mother always has a great menu," Xavier said.

"Delicious items like chili burgers and fries?" she asked, hoping to lighten the mood.

He laughed softly. "Not quite. Today's menu is salad-themed. Wedge salad to start, pasta salad, and similar dishes. Not as good as a chili burger, but still very delicious."

Diana searched his eyes. "What will I wear? Is this a formal event?"

"Informal. Look at what I'm wearing. What did you bring that you could wear?"

"I guess…my white top and black pants."

"That's fine."

"Xavier…"

"Listen to me." He squeezed her hands. "I want you to meet my mother. She's important to me, and you're important to me."

"Why? Give me one good reason why I'm so important."

His mouth twisted upward into affectionate humor. "Because your face is so expressive." He tapped the tip of her nose. "It's cute how you wrinkle your nose when you don't like something, and even when you put that serene expression on your face to hide your thoughts, that tells me plenty." His eyes softened. "I appreciate the way you love your son. Not every woman wants to be a mother and not every woman is cut out to be a mother, but you—it's obvious how much you love Andre and your bond with him reminds me of my relationship with my mother. I don't see a future with any woman who I can't see as the mother of my children." He brought her hand to his lips. "And then there's the fact that you're soft and smell really, really good."

He nibbled the back of her hand, and Diana laughed softly.

"I asked for one good reason and you gave me four."

"I have forty more." Sliding his hands to her hips, he pulled her closer so their bodies were flush against each other. "I'll give you the entire list on the ride to my mother's house. What do you say? Come with me."

Diana couldn't fight him anymore, nor, truthfully, did she want to. She wanted to meet his mother and take their relationship to the next level. All she had to do was let go of her fears.

She dropped her forehead to his chest.

"All right, Xavier. I'll do it."

CHAPTER TWENTY-TWO

Diana's choice of outfit definitely pleased Xavier. His eyes lit up once she was fully dressed in the strapless white top, black slacks, and black sandals that showed off her red-painted toenails.

"Where'd you get this?" he asked.

She preened under his hungry gaze. She'd purchased the top with him in mind.

"At Torrid Ashley. It's a plus-size boutique where I do a lot of my shopping."

"Did you get the yellow dress you wore in Missouri there?"

"Yes, and the fuchsia dress I wore to Trenton's wedding."

His dark eyes lit up. "Oh yeah, I loved the way that dress hugged your ass."

"I remember," she said.

"Keep shopping at Torrid Ashley."

She giggled. "Like I said before, you're good for my ego."

Xavier dropped several kisses on her bare shoulders. She laughingly reminded him they were running late, and shoved him toward the front door.

Attending a luncheon at Constance Johnson's house was the easy part, if Diana only had to meet his mother. But such was not the case. When they arrived at the expansive estate, they came in contact with other members of the family she knew from the office.

The head of the company, Cyrus, was already there with his wife Daniella—a model-thin woman wearing a strapless colorful maxi dress that hung loosely over her swollen belly. Ivy Johnson, who oversaw the entire restaurant group, was in attendance with her fiancé—a *New York Times* bestselling author whose nonfiction novel, *The Rules of Man*, was on Diana's to-be-read list. Even more awkward, Trenton, her direct supervisor, was also there with his new wife, Alannah.

The three couples were standing out on the columned loggia. The idyllic location offered great views of the sparkling lake and overlooked a tiered backyard with a lush green lawn and perfectly formed bushes that must require an army of landscapers to maintain. The beautifully set table contained white linens and a centerpiece of red roses that looked like fresh cuts from the garden below.

When Trenton saw Diana, he paused with a glass of lemonade on the way to his mouth. "Diana?" His gaze jumped from her to Xavier and back again.

The three couples stared, and Diana wanted to fall through the floor.

Before she or Xavier could respond, a friendly but dignified female voice with a slight Texas twang came from the right. "Hello," she said, and Diana turned to face the matriarch of the family. She'd come from behind and wore a pleasant expression in pearls, a print top, and white pants. "I'm Constance Johnson, and you must be Diana. Welcome." She took one of Diana's hands in both of hers, relaxing her with the warm clasp.

"Thank you."

"Your face is familiar to me," Constance said slowly.

"Hello, Mother. Sorry we're late," Xavier interjected. He kissed his mother on the cheek. "You probably recognize her because she was at the wedding."

"And she's my executive assistant," Trenton added, in a somewhat resentful tone.

"Oh." Constance's eyes sparkled with interest. "Well, it's a pleasure to meet you. How long have you worked at Johnson Enterprises?"

"Over three years. I've worked for Trenton for two."

"Lovely." Her kind eyes looked steadily into Diana's as she continued to gently hold her hand. "I'm sure Xavier explained my rules to you, but in case he didn't, I don't allow business talk at the table. So we'll have to find more interesting topics to discuss. And you will sit next to me, so I can get to know you better." She patted Diana's hand.

Nervous energy took root in her stomach. Oh, boy. Xavier was close with his mother and had a high opinion of her.

A young girl wearing glasses came running onto the loggia. Diana recognized her as Katie, Ivy and Lucas's eleven-year-old daughter.

"Auntie Terri and Uncle Gavin are here with the new baby!" she announced, bouncing up and down on her toes.

Terri appeared first with blonde braids that extended to her elbows. She wore a red caftan with a gold pattern and carried a baby boy in a blue-and-white blocked blanket. A nanny followed, pushing a double stroller with the sleeping twins—Elisabeth and Gavin, Jr.— and Gavin pulled up the rear.

The family members crowded around Terri and the newborn while Gavin eased out of the way.

"Diana," he said, eyebrows raised in surprise.

"Hello, Gavin."

Xavier placed an arm around her shoulders in a protective stance.

"Congratulations," Diana said to Gavin, folding her hands together in front of her.

"Thank you." He beamed.

Cyrus, the eldest, broke away from the group fawning over the newest addition to the family, and walked over. "Can I talk to you for a minute?" he said to Xavier.

Right away, Diana felt the tension in Xavier's body.

"Cyrus—"

"Just for a few." The firm tone indicated he wouldn't take no for an answer.

"I'll be right back," Xavier said to Diana, hesitating, his eyes searching her face.

While she was certain he wouldn't leave if she gave any indication she was uncomfortable being left alone, she determined to handle the situation. She didn't need to be coddled, and as much as she appreciated him, she could stand on her own two feet.

"Go ahead. I'll be fine. While you're gone, I'll have a chance to love on the baby, too."

"I'll only be gone a few minutes," he promised. She watched him walk away, and when Constance beckoned to her, she joined the family surrounding Terri and the baby.

****

Xavier turned on Cyrus in the sunroom. "Before you start—"

"What are you thinking about, dating an employee?" Cyrus demanded. "That's a recipe for disaster."

"Cyrus—"

"You're the COO of the company. Do you understand the liability you're exposing us to by sleeping with an executive assistant? The scandal that could result if your fling doesn't work out?"

Xavier bristled. "It's not a fling."

"Then what is it?"

"We're in a relationship. I wouldn't have brought her here if she wasn't important to me."

Cyrus ran a hand over the back of his head. "That's all well and good, but did you consider the power dynamics of your relationship?"

"Of course I did, but nothing you say will change my mind."

"I didn't think I could and that wasn't my intention, but you should think about the ramifications of your actions and how you're going to handle the end of this relationship. Frankly, it could blow up in your face. We had one catastrophe last year—or did you forget?"

"I didn't forget."

Last year, a mid-level manager had been involved in an extramarital affair with a clerk in his department.

"There are some important differences here," Xavier said. "The clerk said she felt pressured to sleep with him to keep her job, that the sexual encounters weren't consensual."

"And he says they were."

"You're also forgetting I'm not Diana's direct supervisor," Xavier pointed out.

"Oh well, wonderful, then by all means, work your way through the entire roster of employees." Cyrus spoke through his teeth, and despite the fact that his anger was understandable, Xavier had absolutely no regrets. "As the second-in-command, *everyone* is your direct report."

Trenton and Gavin came into the room and Xavier lifted his eyes heavenward. "Don't start."

"What are you doing with my assistant?" Trenton asked. "Could you have at least given me fair warning?"

Gavin crossed his arms over his chest. "He's been doing his own thing a lot lately."

Xavier glared at him. "The decision to bring her to the luncheon was last-minute, and not that it's any of your business, but I genuinely care about Diana. We're seeing each other, and that's not going to change. You'll all have to get used to it."

"Don't we have a policy against this kind of thing?" Trenton asked.

"The company policy *discourages* relationships between supervisors and subordinates. Relationships are not *prohibited*, and I'm not her supervisor."

"Somebody's been studying the sexual harassment policy," Gavin murmured.

Xavier glared at his brother again. "Yes, Gavin, I have. Believe me, I don't want a scandal any more than you all do."

The four of them fell quiet, an uncomfortable silence filling the room.

Finally Trenton spoke up. "I like Diana and she's an excellent assistant. I don't want to lose her when your relationship goes south."

"Why does everyone think our relationship won't last?" Xavier demanded, offended by the prevalent doubt.

"You haven't been with anyone since you moved back, and you haven't exactly been known to stay in long-term relationships," Cyrus pointed out.

"Because the volunteer work I did for years wasn't conducive to having a long-term relationship," Xavier said between his teeth. Traveling to various communities over short spans of time, many of them in rural or remote areas, didn't allow him to foster romantic relationships. "For the record, I've dated several women since I've been back, but I chose not to share my relationships with you three."

Gavin's eyebrows raised while Cyrus and Trenton stared.

"Why all the secrecy?" Cyrus asked.

"I don't know." Xavier paced over to the window, which looked onto the lake. He swung around. "Actually, I do know. None of them—for various reasons—were wife material for me. It's as simple as that. So I didn't see the point of discussing them, and certainly didn't see the point of bringing them to meet Mother."

"Well, damn, this sounds serious," Gavin said.

Xavier conceded that his brother was right. Verbalizing his feelings had made them all the more concrete. He'd come to depend on his relationship with Diana. It made his day when he heard her voice or saw her face. He looked forward to their time together, and bringing her to meet the family indicated how important she'd become to him. This relationship was special. Different. He wanted it to work.

Ivy appeared in the doorway. "Mother sent me to remind you that we have a guest, and she wants your presence right away at the table." Her gaze traveled over the four of them. "What did I miss?"

"Nothing," Xavier answered, heading for the door.

"Why don't you guys tell me anything?" she demanded.

"Because you talk too much." Gavin flung his arm around his twin's neck. Ivy had a habit of confiding in their mother, even when they told her not to. "Don't worry, I'll update you later," he said in a stage whisper.

"You better."

****

Lunch turned out not to be as stressful as Diana anticipated. When the men returned, their subdued airs suggested they'd had an important conversation, and she knew it concerned her and Xavier. What helped to put her at ease more than anything was Constance's kind nature and Terri, who sat to her left.

While Diana tried not to gawk at the team of servants bringing out platters of food and serving beverages, Terri—still cradling her new baby—leaned sideways and whispered, "You'll get used to it. It's overwhelming at first, but the family's great. Very down-to-earth, considering. You may have the most down-to-earth member of the bunch. I love my husband, but Gavin has led a very privileged life, and sometimes it shows."

"I heard my name," he said from across the table.

"I'm saying good things," Terri said, blowing him a kiss.

"Uh-huh." He grinned at her.

And with that, the conversation flowed around them. Diana learned a lot that day. Alannah and Trenton shared the details of their trip to the Taj Mahal and the serenity of Thailand, where they soaked up the rays at their villa's private pool, walked hand in hand along the beach, and participated in the nightlife. Lucas gave an update on the budding relationship with his mother, whom he'd connected with in Panama. She'd been a teen mother and given him up, running down to Central America to stay with relatives a few years later—where she'd lived since.

Jokes were made about how many more children Terri and Gavin were going to have. Constance made it clear she expected more grandchildren—from all her children.

"I think eight is a nice, round number," Gavin teased, winking at his wife across the table.

"Eight total?" Terri said. "From all of us?"

"No, eight from you and me."

"Um, no, and those two are next." Terri pointed at Alannah and Trenton.

Alannah, a freckle-faced beauty with an air of innocence, said to her best friend, "Hey, don't rush us."

Katie piped up. "I want a lot more cousins and a baby brother!"

"The pressure's on," Daniella warned Ivy.

"Tell me about it. She's been begging for a baby brother for the past two years. Now that we've found Lucas's parents, we can finally move forward with our wedding plans." Her eyes found her fiancé's.

"And a baby brother!" Katie added, pumping her hands above her head.

The family erupted into laughter, and Diana, feeling much more relaxed than when she first arrived, joined in. The Johnsons made a point of pulling her into the conversation, asking questions about her son and family. She realized and appreciated that they were doing their best to make her feel welcomed and at ease.

It was only later, after Constance had given her a hug and kiss good-bye, and she and Xavier were driving back in the car, that Diana digested the importance of the visit to his mother's home.

"Thank you for inviting me," she said, reaching for his hand.

He glanced away from the road. "Did you enjoy yourself?"

"I did. It was nice getting to know your family outside of the office."

They were an interesting bunch, and from being in their company in that setting, Diana gained a new appreciation of the Zambian proverb on Xavier's back: *A tree is strong because of its roots.*

The visit demonstrated how seriously he took their relationship. Now it was time for her to do the same for him. Keeping her gaze on his strong profile, Diana said quietly, "I'd like you to meet Andre."

He glanced away from the road and looked deeply into her eyes. "I'd like to meet him, too."

CHAPTER TWENTY-THREE

Xavier collected all of the contract copies from Jaclyn and laid them on the oval table at one end of his office. While he worked, Gavin entered.

His brother stood back and folded his arms over his chest, taking a good look at Xavier. "You're going to stay calm during this meeting, right?"

Leading up to this final meeting, Xavier had become even more upset when it became clear the unethical steps Nathan Morse and his brothers had taken to "cook the books." They created fictitious accounts and false sales to show money owed to the company that didn't exist. Fake invoices, fake addresses, and even fake websites, were created to fool the auditors. Fortunately, Nathan had made the mistake of responding to the sample of accounts receivables inquiries with 100 percent accuracy, which set off a red flag.

Investigators had tracked down the alleged businesses. One was an empty parking lot. Another a roadside restaurant. By the end of the investigation, it appeared that approximately half of the assets they claimed were deemed to be fraudulent. Meanwhile, Nathan and his brothers had been skimming money from the till.

"I'll keep calm, as long as Nathan does what he's supposed to do, which is sign on the line."

"Where do you need me and what to do you want me to do?" Gavin asked.

Xavier set a pen on the table, in front of the chair he expected Nathan to occupy. "At the other end of the table, answer the questions he has, and back up our decision."

"Present a united front," Gavin said.

"Exactly."

Minutes later, Nathan and his brother Shane—the company comptroller—were shown into the conference room. His brother was a younger version of Nathan, with the same dark brown hair and clear brown eyes. An older gentleman followed behind with white hair and wearing glasses, introduced as their attorney.

Bringing counsel was a waste of time. Not a single word of the contracts would change. Not even a typo.

After handshakes all around, the five men sat at the oval table with Xavier and Gavin at the long ends.

"How are your daughters?" Gavin asked Nathan.

Nathan, seated to Xavier's left, grinned. His entire face transformed at the mention of the girls. "Haley started dance class two weeks ago and the instructor said she's a natural. Jasmine has decided she wants to be a scientist, so we've had to be extra diligent about keeping products out of her reach. The other day she used a chair to access the hand soap in the bathroom and combined it with aftershave to make an 'experiment.' It was a mess."

They all chuckled, except Xavier. He wasn't in the mood for small talk. Cute anecdotal stories about his daughters aside, Nathan Morse was scum.

"As we discussed on the phone," Xavier said, getting right down to business, "we've significantly lowered our offer price. I shared all of that with you via email, so I understand you're here to sign the final copies." He folded his hands together on the shiny surface of the table.

The room went quiet.

Nathan looked at the attorney seated across from him. Xavier couldn't read the silent message that passed between them, but whatever communication they shared had Nathan straightening in his chair.

"Actually, there are few things we would like to change in the contract. We agree the original asking price might have been a little high. The new offer, however, is significantly lower than we would like."

Shane shifted in his chair. For Xavier, that was an indication he didn't agree with his brother.

"What made you come to that conclusion?" Xavier asked. His body tensed as his anger mounted.

One corner of Nathan's mouth lifted into a sort of smirk. "It's obvious Johnson Brewing Company is still interested. Which means that this deal is still open for negotiation." He sat back and stuck out his chest.

Gavin's gaze met Xavier's, sending a telepathic message that he'd take the lead. "You're mistaken. No part of the offer to purchase is open for negotiation any longer. This is our final offer, which was explained to you in detail over the phone and via email."

This time it was Nathan's lawyer's turn to shift uneasily, but Nathan himself remained relaxed and even laughed. He tapped a finger on the sheets in front of him. "Let's not play games here. I'm not signing this contract, because I don't agree with your offer."

"You and your brothers falsified the information you shared with us while you skimmed money off the profits," Gavin pointed out, irritation slipping into his voice.

Nathan swung his head in Gavin's direction. "It's our company and we can do whatever we want. Despite all that, it's obvious you still want our company. If you want Morse Brewing, you're going to have to pay us a reasonable sum."

"Or what?" Xavier asked. "Once word gets out, no one is going to want to buy the company."

Nathan shrugged. "So you say. But I have solid distribution, contacts, and talented workers, which I know you're very interested in. We chose to work with JBC because of your great reputation, but we have other options."

"We're not changing our offer," Xavier said.

"Then I guess this was a wasted trip. Our business is done here." Nathan nodded across the table and stood. His attorney and brother followed suit.

Gavin and Xavier remained seated, and Xavier's hand fisted on the table.

"You came all the way down here to walk away?" Gavin asked.

"I came all the way down here to negotiate," Nathan said arrogantly. Palms flat, he leaned on the table and swung his head from one end to the next, so both Johnson brothers received his attention. "But you're not in a negotiating mood. You seem to think that because you're the second-largest brewer in the country, you can somehow railroad me. That's not going to happen here today. If you don't offer better terms for Morse Brewing, I'm sure someone else will. Even with the discrepancies on the balance sheets."

"You call flat-out falsifying your assets a discrepancy?" Xavier demanded in a loud voice. This man had balls on him.

"This conversation is over." Nathan's face shifted into hard lines, transforming him into his true character. Someone without a conscience. Someone who didn't care about anyone but himself.

Xavier stood, towering over Nathan.

"Oh shit," Gavin murmured.

"Sit your ass down," Xavier said.

"Excuse me?" Nathan said.

"I said, sit your ass down!"

Shane and the attorney immediately returned their butts to their seats.

Nathan swallowed, his gaze connecting with Xavier's in a battle of wills, but then he seemed to think better of it. He lowered into his chair.

Xavier reclaimed his chair. "Here's what you're going to do," he said calmly and slowly. "You're going to sign this contract, and you're going to sign it for the amount we've offered, and not a penny more. You're correct—we're the second-largest brewing company in the country. Which means we have a lot of influence. No one else will want your garbage company after we get through spreading the word in the industry about your nonexistent assets. Quit bluffing. There are no other offers. This is the best you're going to get."

He leaned forward, getting in Nathan's face. "In case you still think this is optional, if you don't sign, I won't rest until you lose everything you own. Your house. The three high-end cars. The vacation home in Mexico. Everything. Including your girlfriend's St. Louis apartment."

Nathan's eyes widened.

That little bit of information had been a true shocker because Nathan portrayed the image of being a devoted family man married to his high school sweetheart. Meanwhile, he owned a condo where he kept a mistress.

The other man's jaw tightened. "You wouldn't."

"I have nothing to lose. You're the one with your business, livelihood, and family at stake." Xavier tapped the copies in front of Nathan with a forefinger. "Sign."

"Sign the damn contract and let's get out from under this thing. Their offer is the best we're going to get," Shane said.

"Listen to your brother." Xavier set his phone on the table and turned on the timer to sixty seconds. "For every minute that passes where you don't sign, the offer drops by ten percent."

Shane's eyes opened wide. "For God's sake, Nathan, sign the damn contract!"

Mouth set in a firm, taut line, Nathan dragged the stack of papers toward him. He made a big show of picking up the pen, glared at Xavier, but started signing.

Xavier turned off the timer and watched as he signed and initialed everywhere his endorsement was needed.

****

As his housekeeper said, Xavier found Cyrus on the rooftop with his son, Michael. The toddler sat at a Sesame Street table doing the worst coloring job ever with only a red crayon. Cyrus looked on, feet propped on a low table in front of the unlit outdoor fireplace, a bottle of water on a table next to him. In the distance, the Space Needle glowed like a beacon in the night.

"What's going on, Michael?" Xavier dropped a kiss to the top of his nephew's head and fell into the seat catty-corner to his brother. He set a bottle of beer on the floor of the rooftop. Cyrus didn't drink, but he kept alcoholic beverages available for guests.

Michael looked up, grinned, and replied in the unintelligible language toddlers sometimes spoke that only their parents understood.

"Are you being a good boy?" Xavier asked.

Michael nodded his head vigorously. "Good boy." He then concentrated on the coloring book again.

"No, he's not," Cyrus said. "He's been cranky and crying most of the night because he misses his m-o-m-m-y."

Xavier stretched out his legs. "Where is she?"

"At her New York gallery taking care of some business. She'll be back tomorrow. He should be asleep right now, but he screamed and cried when the nanny tried to put him down, so I brought him up here with me."

"Sounds like he's stubborn."

"He is." Cyrus sounded more proud than disgruntled.

"Wonder where he gets that from."

Cyrus chuckled. "I wouldn't know."

Michael hopped up from the table and took the coloring book with him to Cyrus. "Look, Daddy. Pwetty."

Cyrus held the book and gave his son's work serious consideration. "Yes, it's very pretty. Good job. Do another one."

"Okay." Michael lumbered back to the table, flipped the page, and started on another masterpiece.

"So, how'd the meeting go? I know that's why you're here," Cyrus said.

"Contracts are signed and ready for your signature in the morning."

"How much?" Xavier gave Cyrus the final figure and his eyebrows lifted a half-inch. "That's a steal. You went even lower than we discussed."

"They didn't have a choice, and Nathan knew if we walked away, they couldn't find another buyer. The state their company was in, they were on the verge of bankruptcy."

"Good job."

"Thanks."

Cyrus watched him in silence.

"What?" Xavier said.

"Have you finally accepted who you are yet?"

"What are you talking about?"

"Have you finally accepted that you're more like Father than you realized?"

"One incident doesn't make me like him."

"Agreed, but I noticed the similarities a long time ago."

"When?"

"During that fiasco in Senegal, for instance. The passion with which you defended those people was—well, not the way that I would have handled the situation, but admirable."

"Couldn't tell the way you yelled at me over the phone."

"I was worried. Mother was worried."

"I thought for sure you'd leave me there," Xavier said with a chuckle.

Cyrus frowned. "Tell me you're kidding."

"Sort of. We didn't exactly get along for a while."

Cyrus seemed deep in thought as he watched his son color. "We didn't get along, but you're my brother. There was never any question of whether or not I would help you get out of prison. It was simply a matter of how quickly we could get you out of there. There was a lot of red tape, and you didn't exactly help our efforts by refusing to leave unless the other rioters were released, too."

"I couldn't leave them there." He felt guilty for his role in the outcome, but his feelings went deeper than that. As a Johnson, he'd learned at a young age that loyalty to family was paramount. The Senegalese community were his people—his family.

"Daddy." Michael pouted and rubbed his eyes.

Cyrus held out his hands, and the little boy stumbled to him. Cyrus lifted him against his torso, and Michael laid his head on his father's shoulder, pressing his face into his neck.

A hollow ache filled Xavier's chest. One day he hoped to have that type of relationship—that bond with his own children. A wife to wake up next to and a family to care for. He'd been longing for that for quite some time.

"I understood about having to get them out, too," Cyrus said, "but it complicated your release, for sure."

"You did it, though."

"Yeah." He patted and then rubbed his son's back.

Cyrus and Xavier were silent for a while.

Xavier sipped his beer. "Remember how Father always used to say, 'Sink or swim. Nobody's going to give you anything in this world. Sink or swim.'"

Cyrus laughed. "He meant it literally, too."

Xavier knew exactly what Cyrus was talking about. "That day at the pool," he said.

Cyrus nodded, looking off into the distance.

Their father had stood on the side of the pool and tossed them both in, insisting they'd taken enough swimming lessons and should know what to do.

"How old were we?" Xavier asked.

"I was seven, so you were six," Cyrus answered.

"I thought I was going to die that day." Xavier leaned his head back and stared up at the black sky. Scattered stars twinkled back at him.

"But you didn't," Cyrus said.

He rolled his head to look at Cyrus. "Because you held my hand. Calmed me down."

Cyrus rubbed his son's back and soft snores came from the tiny body. "We're brothers. We're supposed to be there for each other. Besides, do you really think Father would have let anything happen to either of us? Mother would have killed him."

Xavier laughed. "True. Although I didn't think about it at the time. My only concern was surviving."

"If you're not part of the solution…" Cyrus started, using another one of their father's quotes.

"…you're part of the problem. You can't be both," Xavier finished. "We should write down his sayings. Father had a bunch of them."

"He sure did," Cyrus said in a low voice.

Xavier swallowed past the thickness in his throat. He knew they both felt the void their father's death had left.

"I know you didn't push so hard for Morse Brewing because it was a great deal," Cyrus said. "You wanted to make sure those people didn't lose their jobs. It worked out this time, but it won't always. You can't save everyone."

Xavier eyed his brother. "I know. Doesn't mean I can't try."

Cyrus chuckled. "Yeah, you're definitely more like Father than you realize." He was quiet for a few seconds before he turned to Xavier again. "About Diana, I didn't—"

"Don't worry about it, I know you had to say something. We're good." Cyrus took his responsibility of taking care of the family and their reputation very seriously. Xavier didn't always agree with him, but he knew his brother's concerns came from a good place.

He picked up his beer and held the bottle aloft to Cyrus. Cyrus picked up his water and they tapped the bottles together. An instance of understanding had emerged between them.

CHAPTER TWENTY-FOUR

"I never see you anymore." Camille pouted, leaning against the doorjamb of Diana's bathroom as she packed a toiletry bag with items she'd need for the next couple of days.

"You're seeing me now," Diana said.

"I'm happy for you, but I miss you." Camille crossed her arms.

"Awww." Diana went over to her cousin and pulled her into a tight hug. "We'll have to do something together soon. Just the two of us." She went back to the counter to finish packing.

"So, things are normal between the two of you?" Camille asked.

Diana zipped up the small bag. "Very normal. Wonderfully normal."

She and Xavier spent time together after hours but kept their distance at work. The lightness of being she experienced with him was unprecedented. There were times she had to pinch herself to make sure she wasn't dreaming. They were compatible in ways she and Rodrick never had been. Nothing about their relationship felt forced or unnatural, and it wasn't just the sex. They laughed at the same jokes. Enjoyed the same food.

The conversation with her son had been interesting to listen to when she'd introduced them. As she stood near the staircase out of sight, they both sat on the stairs and Xavier spoke solemnly to Andre as the 'man of the house.'

"*You like my mommy?*" *Andre asked cautiously.*

"*I do. I like her a lot.*"

"*Do you kiss her?*"

"*Sometimes.*"

Andre didn't reply, but she imagined he must have wrinkled his nose because Xavier laughed.

"*Grown-ups do that sometimes,*" *he explained.* "*Your mommy is very important to me, and I know you're very important to her. I want to get to know you better, if that's okay.*"

There was a moment of silence. "*Yeah, that's okay. I don't mind, but you have to be nice to her.*"

"*I promise to be nice.*"

"*And you won't make her cry?*"

Diana's heart melted.

"*I won't make her cry,*" *Xavier promised.*

From that day, their relationship slowly progressed, and Xavier fostered the closeness with her son by having Andre join them for dinner or weekend trips to the market. He invited them both to a party on his family's boat. With plenty of food, drinks, and games, it was an experience Andre still talked about weeks later. He and Xavier had reached the point now where they shared inside jokes and Xavier was teaching her son to juggle.

"You can't stop smiling when you talk about him," Camille observed, backing up so Diana could pass.

Diana dropped onto the side of the bed. "I wish I'd met Xavier before Rod, but then I wouldn't have my little man."

"And he wasn't exactly available, living halfway across the world in remote villages and whatnot."

Diana laughed. "True."

Camille stuck her hands in the back pockets of her jeans. "Maybe it's for the best. You might not appreciate your relationship as much with Xavier if you didn't know how bad things could be."

"Where is all this wisdom coming from? I'm the older one."

"I give great advice, but I still can't find a job." Camille sighed.

"If you'd let me put in a good word for you, you could probably find a position at Johnson Enterprises. Even if it's entry-level, there's plenty of opportunity for growth."

"That's a last resort. I want to find a job on my own."

Diana nodded her understanding. Camille had been coddled for much of her life, and Diana respected her tenacity and independent streak.

"Still keeping your relationship a secret from you-know-who?" Camille asked.

"For now."

She didn't want to deal with her ex. She already felt guilty for hooking up with Xavier in the house. When she'd told her cousin, Camille had been surprised she'd crossed that line, but making love to Xavier here had been such a freeing act—as if she'd exorcised a ghost or freed herself from iron shackles. Sex that day had been spontaneous and raunchy, and everything she'd hoped sex could be. She'd slept like a baby that night, satiated with pleasure.

"I better get out of here." She hopped up from the bed and picked up her overnight bag. "I'll see you later."

"Bye, hot mama," Camille teased.

Diana gave her hips an extra switch and bounce as she exited.

****

Diana angled her body over the counter, plucking her eyebrows in Xavier's bathroom mirror.

Last night they'd attended a play, but today stayed in to enjoy a lazy Sunday at his house, relaxing.

She'd showered earlier when he went into the home gym. Wearing only a blue cheeky and a blue-and-white pajama top which he never wore, Diana watched Xavier step out of the glass-enclosed shower with a white towel wrapped around his trim waist. The contrast of the towel right next to the dark brown of his skin gave his ribbed abs a darker hued appearance.

Goodness, he's fine.

162

Her eyes traveled over his muscular body. He was so nice to look at, certainly the most good-looking man she'd ever been involved with. Sometimes she simply stared at him, admiring the strength in his jaw, the broad forehead, and his fit, muscular physique.

"So are you going to let me shave you today?" she asked.

"I don't think it's a good idea." He walked over to where she stood in front of the Jack and Jill vanity.

"Why not?" Diana put down the tweezers and examined her work.

"I've never let a woman shave me before, and I don't intend to start now."

Completely serious, he leaned closer to the mirror and rubbed a hand over his whiskered jaw.

She'd already placed all the items she needed on the counter—a silver bowl with warm water, a razor, a washcloth and towel, shaving gel, and aftershave moisturizer.

She picked up the badger brush and waved it at him. "Trust me, I know what I'm doing."

Xavier eyed her skeptically. "Give me that." He reached for the brush but she pulled back.

"I understand this is a process and has to be done right, and I know how to do it."

"I seriously doubt that." He raised a skeptical eyebrow, but at least he hadn't yanked away the brush.

"I do. I know all about not shaving too close to the skin so you won't have ingrown hairs. Etc., etc."

He glowered at her. "There's no etc., etc. You could really mess up my face."

"Trust me. I'm good. Sit." She pointed toward the stool she'd dragged into the bathroom.

What she didn't tell him was that before she married Rodrick, she'd had a boyfriend who frequently let her shave him and she'd enjoyed the experience. Shaving a man was a very intimate act, and she wanted to share the same with Xavier.

He kept his gaze on her a little longer before grunting his acquiescence. "Don't cut me," he muttered.

"Shush." Their banter entertained her. It was like they'd been together forever. This type of playfulness and intimacy was exactly what she'd craved.

"Let me prep my face," Xavier said.

He rubbed a facial scrub into his jaw and chin to get rid of the dead skin cells and soften the hairs on his face, and then rinsed it away with warm water before taking a seat.

Diana stood between his open legs and smoothed on the shaving gel with the brush, lathering the solution over his cheeks, jaw, and neck. Then, using long downward strokes, she glided the razor lightly through the lather and avoided the circle of hair around his mouth. She sensed the tension in him, sitting stiffly in the chair, but he allowed her to work. As he became more relaxed, the tension eased from his shoulders and he moved his hands from resting on his own thighs to her hips.

"No touching while I'm working," Diana said.

"Can't help it," Xavier replied, making an effort to move only his lips. "You're so close and these pretty thighs are *right there*." Xavier cupped the exposed underside of her bottom in the revealing panties, and then glided his hands down her thighs. "Nipples all in my face. I'm only a man."

"A man with lack of self-control," she admonished, angling the razor over the curve of his other cheek.

"It's your fault for walking around dressed like this. You're nothing but temptation."

"Is that what I do? Tempt you?"

She concentrated on the work, but felt his gaze as she moved slowly along his jawline.

"Yes, that's what you do."

She continued with slow, steady movements. "Stop talking or you'll end up getting cut." She worked around his circle beard, and between strokes, rinsed the blade with the warm water sitting in the silver bowl. "There. All finished." Only thin streaks of white foam remained. She stepped away and let him splash cool water on his cheeks and jaw.

"Not bad." He examined his face from all angles, smoothing a hand over the hairless skin.

"Told you I'm good," Diana said, one hand on her hip, a cocky tilt to her chin.

Xavier blotted his face dry and added the moisturizing lotion. "I'm going to get spoiled from all this attention," he said, rubbing the product into his face and down his neck. The cool scent of lime and menthol filled the bathroom.

"I don't mind doing it," Diana said.

Their eyes connected in the mirror. When he'd finished with his face, he took a seat on the stool again and pulled her between his legs. He ran his fingertips over the back of her hands.

"You look like you want to say something," she said.

She stepped closer and placed one of his hands on her hip. She always craved his touch. She ran a hand over his shoulder. He felt smooth as silk but firm as stone.

"I want to tell you how I feel, but I don't want you to freak out."

She stopped moving her hand. "Oh?" Her stomach painfully contracted.

He looked deeply into her eyes. "I love you."

Diana's heart jumped and her hand fell away.

"What are you thinking?"

"I don't know what to think." She swallowed the pounding fear slithering up her throat. "I expected you to say that, but you still took me by surprise." She laughed out of awkwardness.

"I've been thinking about my feelings for a while." One hand glided up her pelvis and his fingers spread over her thick waist.

Diana stared down at the towel he wore. This was what she'd wanted. A solid relationship with a man who adored her.

"You're special to me, Diana."

Her eyes flicked upward to his at the grave tone of his voice.

"I'm overwhelmed. I can't tell you how *good*"—she laughed softly—"which is a lame, inadequate word—you make me feel. You make me feel so good, when for so long I felt like there was something wrong with me." She whispered the words.

"Whatever your ex said is irrelevant." A muscle in his jaw ticked. He stood and edged her backward to the vanity, caging her between the muscular planks that were his arms. "I love you. And I love your son, too."

Her heart stopped.

"And you love me," he continued. "You can deny it, but I know the truth. So are we going to continue to act like this isn't happening?"

Diana licked her lips. "I don't think that would be wise."

"I don't think so, either."

"I'm scared."

"Don't be scared. I won't hurt you, and I'll never let anyone hurt you."

"Promise?"

"Promise."

He dipped his head to kiss her. Their mouths lingered against each other in an intimate caress. Her lips trembled in an excited quiver.

Placing one arm around his neck, Diana threw her whole body into the kiss, pressing against him. Her other hand dragged across his chest and rubbed one of his nipples. He groaned and lifted his head, and she lifted onto her toes, loathe to lose contact.

Xavier set his forehead against hers. "I love you. Don't ever doubt that, okay?"

She gave a faint nod, and he nipped her bottom lip. Then he sucked her chin and then her neck, sending coils of heat to her groin.

She loosened the knot in the towel and it fell to the tile floor. Xavier picked her up and set her on the vanity.

"I love you," she whispered close to his mouth.

"I know, sweetheart," he said against her lips.

Fisting a hand in his dreadlocks, she dragged his mouth back to hers. Easing up from the countertop, she allowed him to slip the panties down her thighs.

Pulses pounding, hearts singing, they made sweet, passionate love as they whispered words of love and affection to each other.

CHAPTER TWENTY-FIVE

Diana's eyes fluttered open.

What caused her to wake up?

Her ears picked up a faint buzzing sound that repeated over and over until she realized that it was her phone vibrating. Groaning, she rolled out of Xavier's arms and reached for her purse on the nightstand. When she retrieved the phone, she saw her ex-husband's number on the screen.

"Hello?"

"Where the hell have you been?" Rodrick demanded.

Raising onto an elbow, Diana squinted into the darkness. Worry developed in her stomach. "What's wrong?"

"I've been trying to reach you for the past hour. Why haven't you been answering your phone?"

"What is it?" She sat all the way up, panic edging into her voice.

Xavier sat up beside her.

"I'm with Andre at the hospital. He had an allergic reaction to something he ate or touched, I don't know what it is. I rushed him here to the hospital and the doctors gave him some medicine, but his face is damn near disfigured. I don't recognize him." His voice sounded strained and hoarse.

The first time Andre experienced an allergic reaction, Rodrick had been out of town.

"Which hospital are you at?"

"The children's hospital," he told her, sounding less upset, as if knowing she was on her way brought him instant relief. "Are you coming now? He keeps asking for you."

Diana flung back the covers. "I'll be right there." She hung up the phone.

"What's wrong?" Xavier asked.

"My son. He's in the hospital. He had an allergic reaction to something he ate." Even she could hear the shaking in her voice. She flicked on the bedside lamp and started getting dressed. "I have to get out of here. I'm sorry."

"I'm coming with you." Xavier rolled off the bed and searched the floor for his clothes.

"You don't have to do that," Diana said.

"You don't actually think I'm going to let you go to the hospital by yourself, do you?" Frowning at her, he snatched a pair of khakis from the floor.

She wanted him with her, but worried about him meeting Rodrick. "You and Rodrick haven't met. It might be problematic to meet under these circumstances."

"I care about Andre and I'm going to be there for you. Besides, you don't have your car. I picked you up, remember?"

Diana straightened the floral print dress and picked up her purse. "I can call a car or catch a cab."

"Or you can stop arguing and let me take you to the hospital."

Xavier pulled a shirt over his head, and Diana barely refrained from running around the foot of the bed and kissing him in gratitude.

Minutes later, they were in his SUV on the way to the hospital. When they arrived, she found her ex-husband in the room with Andre, the lines taut around his mouth. Having been through this before, she knew the doctors would require them to stay for at least a few hours until they were certain Andre was satisfactorily recovering.

When Rodrick looked up and saw her with Xavier, his eyes narrowed and his mouth flattened with displeasure.

"Xavier, this is my ex-husband, Rodrick Cambridge. Rodrick, Xavier Johnson."

"Johnson?" One of Rodrick's eyebrows shot upward.

Xavier extended his hand. "I'm sorry we have to meet under these circumstances."

Rodrick didn't say a word, but shook his hand.

"Mommy," Andre moaned in a pitiful voice. His eyes were swollen shut, his lips blown up to three times their normal size, and his face red and puffy.

"I'm here, baby."

Diana hurried to sit on the side of the bed and pulled her son into her arms. She flipped up his shirt. Hives covered his back and stomach.

"Oh, my poor baby," she murmured, cradling him to her breasts.

"It itches."

Andre scratched his neck, but she eased away his hand. "I know, baby, but don't scratch, okay?"

Andre whimpered.

"Shh."

Xavier came to stand before them. "Hey buddy, it's going to be okay. Listen to your mommy."

"I'm going to get some coffee," Rodrick said.

Diana watched him leave the room. He was definitely not happy.

About an hour later, Andre had dozed off and she asked Xavier to remain in the room with him while she went to talk to her ex.

She found him in the hallway, seated with his eyes closed, a half-empty paper cup of coffee on the floor next to the chair, and the crown of his head touching the wall behind him.

"Rodrick." He opened his eyes. "How did this happen?" She was always extra careful of everything Andre ate and touched.

"What do you care? You were busy with your boyfriend."

The angry tone took her aback. "Of course I care. He's my son, and I want to make sure this doesn't happen again."

"You want to make sure this doesn't happen again, then you should spend more time with your kid. Where were you?" He stood, his stance antagonistic.

"I have him all week and every other weekend. Are you telling me it's too much trouble for you to take him sometimes?"

"I'm telling you that you should have been available. Not off doing whoever or whatever you were doing." His eyes flashed at her. "Xavier this and Xavier that. That's all I've heard from Dre this weekend, and now I find out he's the oh-so-great Xavier Johnson who owns the company where you work. It would have been nice to meet this man who's spending so much time with my son."

"I intended for you to."

"When?"

"When the time was right. I only introduced him to Dre a few weeks ago."

Rodrick grunted. "The real question is, why is he here?"

"No, the real question is, why is Dre here? You know he's allergic to nuts, and you must have exposed him to them somehow. You have to be careful." She didn't want to sound accusatory, but this was a serious matter. If Andre's breathing had been cut off, he could have died. The very thought sent panic clawing at her throat.

"Are you really blaming me for what happened?"

"I'm not blaming you." It was so hard to reason with him about anything. "I'm saying he's a child and not as careful as he needs to be. We, as the adults, have to be diligent."

"If you hadn't been screwing your boyfriend, you could have come sooner, too, couldn't you?"

"Really, Rod? My relationship has nothing to do with you giving him something with nuts in it. What did you give him tonight?"

"What I do with my son on my time is my goddamn business." He walked away from her.

Infuriated, Diana followed. "Why do you have to be so difficult all the damn time? We need to talk about this."

He swung around on her. "I don't have anything to say to you."

"Is this really because of Xavier? I'm allowed to have a life."

"Yes, Diana. You're allowed to be the slut you've always wanted to be. Congratulations. Now you're a rich man's whore."

She cringed at the ugly words. "I won't let you shame me."

"Because you have no shame." He curled his lip at her. "You got this man blowing your head up and now your fat ass think you fine."

Diana recoiled. The words dripped like acid from his tongue and scorched her heart with the same flaming intensity. She glared at Rodrick. "You're just mad because my fat ass doesn't want your trifling, lame—"

He snatched her wrist, the same as he'd done before, and tightened his grip in a merciless squeeze. Dragging her to the end of the hallway, he cowed her against the wall. "Don't get carried away. You want a battle, I can give you one. Remember who holds the deed to the house you live in. I don't have to put up with you."

"So you're going to put your son out on the street?"

"No, I'll put you out on the street and take my son."

Shock reverberated down Diana's spine.

Rodrick's eyes narrowed. "Yeah, you didn't think about that, did you? Obviously you want to spend more time with your boyfriend, so why don't I give you all the time you need? I take full custody of my son, and you get out of my house."

Her throat tightened in panic. "You would never take care of Dre by yourself, twenty-four-seven. You're bluffing."

He brought his face closer to her, lips curled in disgust. "Want to call my bluff?"

She didn't recognize Rodrick with the ugly snarl drawn into his features. What had happened to him? How had he turned into this monster who only wanted to shame and hurt her? Had the signs always been there, but she'd simply missed them? What a transformation from the kind, gentle man she'd fallen in love with.

"I don't know you anymore," she said.

His face blanked for a second, as though the words cut through him. Then a sneer appeared. "And I don't know you. You try to pretend you're so sweet, but let's be real. You're exactly like

172

your father. You get around, you sleep around, and I will not have my son raised by a woman like that."

His hand tightened around her wrist.

"Stop," she said, eyes darting around as she tried not to make a scene. She didn't try to pull away because his fingers would only tighten.

"Andre is my son. *Mine*, do you hear me? I won't be replaced."

"You're his father. No one is trying to replace you."

"No? So you didn't bring your rich boyfriend here to flaunt him as a replacement in my face?"

"I'm not flaunting—"

"Is everything okay?" Xavier's voice came from behind Rodrick.

Her ex-husband stiffened and dropped her hand. With his jaw set in a hard line, he turned to face Xavier with his chest puffed out. "I'm having a conversation with my ex-wife. Is that a problem?"

Xavier's brown eyes filled with steel. "Not a problem at all, if you stick to talking. Looked like more than talking was going on." His gaze dropped to where Diana was rubbing her wrist. "You okay?" The tension in him was almost palpable.

She nodded.

"Andre woke up and asked for you," Xavier said, keeping his eyes on her face.

"Okay." She walked over to stand beside him.

"I was just leaving." Rodrick straightened his shoulders. "I'm sure the two of you can take it from here." He cast a look at Diana. "Think about what I said." He walked down the hallway.

Xavier's hand touched her shoulder. "Diana—"

She moved out of his reach and turned away, blinking back tears. "I'm fine."

Xavier rested his hands on her shoulders. "Sweetheart, look at me."

She took a quivering breath and shook her head.

"Talk to me. What do you need?"

"Nothing right now."

He walked around in front of her and cupped her cheek. "You sure?"

"Could we not do this now, please?" She shrunk away from his touch. "I want to take care of my son."

The conversation with Rodrick was too much to digest on top of making sure Andre was okay, and Andre was her priority. Always.

They watched cartoons with Andre in the room. Neither said much, but Xavier's quiet presence gave her comfort. After a couple more hours, the doctor released Andre into Diana's care. She picked up his book bag, and Xavier lifted him from the bed. Her son hooked his arms around Xavier's neck and settled his head on his shoulder.

"You okay, big guy?" she asked, voice thick with emotion. She patted her son's back.

Andre nodded and closed his eyes. Xavier walked ahead of her, and Diana's heart melted at the sight of him holding her son. Andre looked like little more than a doll against Xavier's big body. For a moment, she thought of the three of them as a unit, a family. But Rodrick's threat burned like acid in her throat.

I'll put you out on the street and take my son.

By the look on his face, this time he meant it.

CHAPTER TWENTY-SIX

Diana jumped when the phone on her desk rang. She'd zoned out again. Pressing a hand to her temple, she answered. "Hi, Trenton."

"Could you come in here for a few minutes? I have something I need to go over with you." He sounded rather solemn.

"Should I bring a notepad?"

"No, just bring yourself." He hung up.

Diana gnawed on her bottom lip, but went into Trenton's office.

"Have a seat." He waved toward one of the chairs in front of his desk and she sat down, clasping her hands together in her lap.

Trenton came around to sit on the edge of the desk. He smiled at her, but there was something a bit unnerving about his expression. It didn't contain the usual friendliness. He appeared benevolent, and her stomach tanked.

"How are things going with you and Andre?" he asked.

"Andre?"

"Yes. When you missed work the other day, you mentioned he'd been in the hospital for an allergic reaction to nuts?"

"Oh, yes." Although Andre had fully recovered by Monday morning, she'd kept him home one more day and called in. Trenton, as usual, had graciously allowed her to miss the day. "He's fine now. Doing a lot better."

175

"Good." He reached behind him and lifted a manila envelope from the desk. "We need to talk about your performance and a few things I've noticed."

Diana swallowed. This didn't sound good. Outside of her annual review, Trenton had never spoken to her about her performance except to say she'd done a good job, but this was clearly not one of those times. Granted, she'd been distracted over the past few days. Rodrick had followed through on his threat and sent an eviction notice, claiming a lease violation for having an extra occupant, Camille.

Soon he'd be ready to fight for custody of Andre, and with his deeper pockets, he could afford better attorneys. She had to find a place to live and soon would have to fight to keep her son. The stress of a pending legal battle gave her a headache.

She waited in silence for Trenton to continue.

"I've noticed your attention to detail is not what it used to be. Nothing too major. A mistake here or there. I figured maybe you were having a tough time with your son. However..." He pulled a stack of pages out of the envelope. "I felt the need to say something this time, because it could potentially affect our business. Do you recognize these?"

Diana nodded. "They're the new contracts you asked me to send to the Fizer Hotel in Las Vegas." The owner didn't like using their document management system where they signed contracts electronically, so she'd had to send out paper contracts to get original signatures.

"That's right. Except these weren't sent to the Fizer Hotel. They were sent to the Intercontinental."

Diana gasped and bolted from the chair. She'd sent confidential contracts to the wrong contact.

"Sit, sit." Trenton kept his voice low and waved her back into her seat.

Diana slowly lowered onto her butt. "I am so sorry. I don't know what's come over me. I've been a little distracted, but that's no excuse." With her concentration in tatters, she'd been making mistakes—careless ones she'd never made before. But this was inexcusable.

"Do you need some time off? Whatever's going on with you, you know that you can come to me and if you need time, you can take it."

It was on the tip of her tongue to deny she needed a break, but then she nodded vigorously. "Yes, I do."

That was the great thing about working for Trenton. He was demanding—which she completely understood for someone with his level of responsibility—but a compassionate supervisor. She took great pride in being dependable and someone he could count on, but this mistake was a black mark against an otherwise stellar record.

"I would like to take tomorrow off but can finish out the day."

His green eyes examined her with concern. "There are only a few more hours left in the day, so why don't you take the rest of the day off, too?"

"Are you sure? Won't you need me?"

"I'm fine, and if anything comes up, I'll get Abigail at the front to assist me. Okay?"

She nodded. "Okay. At least I can mail this out to the proper location before I go." She rose from the chair and took the envelope and contracts from him. At the door, she turned. "Trenton, I'm terribly sorry about this."

He'd already rounded his desk. "Diana, I know you. I know this isn't your usual, so I'm convinced once you take a break, you'll be back to normal, and whatever you're working through will be resolved."

He smiled in a disarming way and she sent a tentative smile back at him before walking out the door.

She'd take him up on his offer to leave and head home because she needed time to think about a decision that had weighed on her mind for the past few days. A decision she could no longer put off.

****

Xavier sat in the driveway of Diana's house, arms folded over the steering wheel, with a nagging sense of déjà vu. The last time a woman had wanted to talk to him, he'd been dumped. Diana's voice held the same underlying note of sadness and resignation he'd recognized in Sasha's voice.

Whereas he'd walked into the restaurant and accepted Sasha's decision, he couldn't do the same with Diana. For that reason, he couldn't move. He stared at the door, coming up with arguments to talk her out of her decision. Whatever she said, he'd argue her down until she changed her mind. It was as simple as that.

He stepped down from the vehicle and rang the doorbell.

Diana opened the door, eyes pink as if she'd been crying. He moved to pull her into his arms, but she withdrew. His chest hitched at her withdrawal.

"Come in," she said woodenly, opening the door wider.

The house was quiet.

"Andre here?" Xavier asked, stepping over the threshold and casting a glance up the stairs. He expected the boy to come bounding down at any minute, like he'd done in the past when he knew Xavier had stopped by.

"I asked Camille to take him to the store so we could be alone to talk." She gestured toward the sofa. "Have a seat."

"No." He took a step forward. "I know what you're about to do, and I want you to listen to me—"

Shaking her head, Diana lifted her hands, palms outward to stop him from touching her. "Please don't make this any more difficult than it has to be." Her eyes pleaded with him. Her big, beautiful eyes which were now filled with sadness.

"What did your ex-husband say to you? I know you're doing this because of something he said the other night at the hospital."

She swallowed. "I told you that my life was complicated."

"And I told you we can work through any complication."

"My son is the most important person in my life. I won't risk losing him."

"Is that what Rodrick threatened you with?"

"He's putting me out of the house and taking Dre because we showed up at the hospital together. He believes that I was rubbing my new relationship in his face and trying to use you to replace him as Andre's father."

"That's ridiculous."

"To you, but not to him. Every move I make, Rodrick thinks it's somehow taking a dig at him."

Xavier flexed his fingers in anger. "Let me talk to him, man-to-man," Xavier said.

Her eyes stretched wider. "No. Absolutely not."

"Why not?"

"Because he wants to make my life a living hell, and having you talk to him will only make the situation worse."

"Your ex feels threatened. It's my fault. I should have...I should have stayed in the car, or..." His voice trailed off in exasperation. He loved her. He loved Andre. There was no way he could have simply dropped her off and driven away. "If you think I'm going to just walk away—"

"Stop! Do you think I want to make this choice—you or my son? I know you want to save me or fix this, but it's too risky. I'm not one of your projects, Xavier. We're talking about my *son*."

"I don't think you're a project," Xavier growled. "I'm partially to blame because of my presence at the hospital, and yes, I want to fix it. I promise you, your situation will not get worse."

"And what if it does? He threatened to file for full custody of Dre."

"He's trying to assert his masculinity by bullying you. He knows he has the upper hand because you're worried about your son. He will not have the upper hand with me."

She crossed her arms over her chest, shutting down. "I've made my decision."

"We moved fast and now you're panicking, but if you stop for a moment and think before making a hasty decision—"

"Xavier, I have to do this. We have to stop seeing each other."

"For how long?"

"Indefinitely."

"Indefinitely?" Xavier repeated, cold fear trickling down his spine. "What does that mean?"

"You know what indefinitely means."

"No way. We love each other."

"I need you to respect my wishes," she said quietly.

"And if I don't?"

"If you don't, and you cause me to lose my son, I'll never forgive you."

They stared at each other and he knew she meant it. One of the characteristics he'd loved so much about Diana was her utter devotion to her son. She was the kind of woman he wanted to be the mother of his own children. So he understood her decision, even as it created a gut-wrenching pain in his chest.

Xavier slowly nodded his head. "All right, then. Understood."

He turned on his heels and walked out.

CHAPTER TWENTY-SEVEN

He may say that he loves you. Wait and see what he does for you.
                                        – Senegalese proverb

The offices of Cambridge Real Estate were located in a ten-story brick building in downtown Ballard, a short drive from Seattle. After making an appointment, Xavier stopped by after work.

He left his jacket in the car and wore only a black vest and striped tie over an arctic blue shirt. In the cabin of the elevator, he watched the numbers climb, taking him to the top floor to Rodrick's office.

No way he could allow Diana's ex to get away with what he was doing to her, and no way he could allow his actions to hurt anyone else he cared about. He may not have been able to help those people in Senegal, but he could help the woman he loved.

In the lobby of Rodrick's office, the receptionist's eyes widened when she saw Xavier, clearly recognizing him.

"Hello, may I help you?"

He nodded. "I have a meeting with Rodrick Cambridge. Xavier Johnson is the name."

"No problem. Let me check." After a quick phone call, she said, "Mr. Cambridge is expecting you. Please have a seat and his assistant will be out in a few minutes."

It took twenty. Having to wait so long annoyed him, but Xavier kept his temper in check and stood when the assistant, a petite, conservatively-dressed woman who looked to be in her mid-forties, approached. She led him down a quiet hallway to the back of the building where a half-open door led into Rodrick's office. She knocked quietly and Rodrick looked up, standing when Xavier entered. The woman excused herself and closed the door behind him.

"I appreciate you seeing me on such short notice," Xavier said.

"No problem. Have a seat." Rodrick waved toward a chair.

"I'd rather stand, if you don't mind. I won't be staying long."

Rodrick smirked. "Okay, let's get down to business. You asked me not to say anything to Diana, so I can guess why you're here, but why don't you tell me."

"I'm here to talk to you about Diana and Andre. She told me what happened, and as you can imagine, it's upsetting to me that my relationship with her has caused her so much distress."

"And you're here to save the day, am I right?"

Xavier allowed a modest smile to cross his lips. "I'm not here to save the day. I'm no hero, but I do want to talk to you about the situation. Diana and I have decided to take a break."

One of Rodrick's eyebrows lifted. "Oh really? What brought that on?" he asked, sounding smug and satisfied.

"Some complications arose, and we decided to go our separate ways."

Rodrick's eyes narrowed. "Huh. So then why are you here?"

"Because first of all, I want you to know that I had no intention of coming between you and your son."

"That's good, because you can't."

A beat passed. Xavier slow-counted to three, letting his temper lower before continuing. "I have a tight-knit family, and I enjoy children. I have a few nieces and nephews, so I'm very comfortable around children and I enjoyed spending time with Andre. He's a good kid."

Rodrick didn't reply, keeping his face cloaked in stoicism.

"The second reason I'm here is to discuss Diana's living arrangements with you. I want to make you an offer on the house."

A dark brow lifted. "The house is not for sale."

"It's not for sale now, and I understand that. But I'm willing to make you a generous offer. I brought my checkbook." Xavier tapped his left breast pocket.

"The house is paid for, and it has sentimental value. I'm not selling it."

"I'm willing to offer you twice what it's worth." Xavier withdrew the appraisal he'd had done on the property and set it on the desk, facing Diana's ex.

Rodrick's suspicious eyes flicked over the report, but he didn't touch it. "I don't want your money. You Johnsons think you can buy whatever you want—land, businesses, people, but you can't buy me. My house is not for sale, and quite frankly, I'd considered withdrawing the eviction notice, but after your visit today, I've changed my mind. I'm tired of taking care of Diana and her no-good cousin anyway."

Xavier ground his teeth.

"Unfortunately for you, I am a Johnson, and I am used to having my way." He chuckled softly. "The older I get, the more I realize my father was more right than he was wrong. He used to say, good behavior may make you a better person, but it will never win you the war." When Rodrick frowned, he continued. "I can't allow you to hurt Diana." He walked over to the window and looked down at the cars and pedestrians in the street. "You're working on a development deal with the Hudson Group, am I right?" From the corner of his eye, he saw Rodrick twist his entire body toward him.

"That's right," he said slowly. Cautiously.

Xavier continued talking to the window, hands tucked into his trouser pockets. "My family knows the Hudsons well. Jake Hudson attended my brother's wedding a few months ago." He turned slowly in Rodrick's direction, whose undivided attention he had now, the smarmy expression gone. "The elder Hudson, the father, was good friends with my father. They used to play golf together. I'm not a golfer myself, but one of my brothers, Cyrus, plays golf with Jake. In fact, when Jake threw a big party the other day, we made sure to send over complimentary cases of our premium beer for his guests." He rubbed his jaw, feigning deep thought. "Have the contracts on the development deal been signed?" He already knew the answer to the question.

"No," Rodrick said shortly.

Xavier could practically see the wheels turning in his head as he considered the loss of millions. He kept his voice neutral, almost friendly. "Listen, I'm not trying to be the bad guy here, but I need you to stop threatening Diana with eviction and the loss of her son. Right now, I'm not angry. But if you continue harassing her, you're going to make me angry."

A beat of silence passed where both men's unwavering gazes remained on each other.

"So what do you propose?"

"I propose you accept my offer of twice what the house is worth so that Diana no longer has to be concerned about where she lives. I also propose that you drop your threats about taking her son away and continue with the shared custody agreement you already have in place."

"And if I don't?"

"If you don't, then we have a problem. I'm a good guy. But I can be a bad guy when I need to be."

Both men stared at each other. Silence filled the room.

With a curt nod, Rodrick made it clear he understood. "Twice the value?"

"That's correct."

With another curt nod, Rodrick indicated his willingness to accept the generous offer.

Xavier withdrew his personal checkbook and wrote in the amount. He signed the check and extended it to Rodrick, and the other man examined the piece of paper the way a jeweler might a potentially fraudulent diamond.

"All this for her?" Rodrick asked, looking up at him.

The hairs on the back of Xavier's neck stood on end. "Pleasure doing business with you." He wouldn't entertain any further conversation with Rodrick. He turned to walk away.

"I can't believe you did all this for that slut. If that's the kind of woman you like, you can have her. But believe me, you'll regret it. She can't be trusted."

This guy...

Xavier had planned to walk out of there without another word, but a surge of fury raged inside of him. People like Diana's ex made it so hard to be good.

"One more thing." He turned and charged toward Rodrick.

Eyes wide, Rodrick shrunk back, but Xavier grabbed him around the neck, twisted his arm behind his back, and slammed him face down onto the desk. He landed with a thud, knocking over a container of pens and pencils and scattering loose papers to the floor. Rodrick squeaked out a whimper and struggled under his grip. He reached backward with the free hand in an effort to hit Xavier, but Xavier dodged the blow and twisted his arm higher. Rodrick let out a pained gasp.

"Stop moving and I won't hurt you anymore than this," Xavier said calmly.

Huffing and puffing, face squinted in pained distress, Rodrick finally realized his actions were in vain. He stopped squirming.

Xavier lowered his head so he could look into the other man's eyes as he lay sprawled atop the desk. "Diana is the mother of your son. Despite the atrocious way you've treated her for years, I've never heard her make one foul comment against you. So when you make any reference to her, you will do so in a respectful manner, showing her the courtesy she deserves. Don't ever call her out her name again. Equally important, if you ever put your fucking hands on her again, I will find you, break every bone in your goddamn body, and then wipe the floor with your shitty face. Are we clear?"

"Yes," Rodrick squeaked out, conversation difficult with his face pressed into the desk.

"Apologize for what you said."

"I'm sorry," he said immediately.

"Tomorrow, you're going to give Diana a call and apologize to her personally for your behavior. You're going to sign over the deed to the house and assure her she no longer has to worry about eviction. You're also going to assure her she no longer has to worry about losing her son. Understood?"

"Yes."

Xavier yanked Rodrick up none too gently from the desk. Shaking, Rodrick backed away, eyes wide and holding onto his arm. A paperclip was stuck to his cheek. "I could sue you for assault."

"You'd have to prove I assaulted you, and if you're foolish enough to make an accusation and sully my family name, I'll bury you and your company so deep you'll wish you'd never heard the name Xavier Johnson. Make sure you deposit that check and get the deed to Diana, or I'll be back." Xavier strolled toward the door. "Good talking to you."

"You're insane!" Rodrick yelled at him as he exited out the door. "You're supposed to be the good one."

CHAPTER TWENTY-EIGHT

She had to do this.

On Saturday morning, Diana stood outside the building that housed Cambridge Real Estate with clammy hands and a thudding heart. She doubted she was making the right decision, but nonetheless, she was ready to fight.

The elevator ride seemed to take forever, but it only took a few minutes. On the tenth floor, she walked confidently over to Rodrick's weekend receptionist.

"Hi Tori, is he still here?"

She and Tori had gotten along well when she worked at the company, and she'd given Diana the go-ahead to come up.

Tori nodded. "Go on back," she whispered.

"Thanks, girl. I owe you one." She would tell Rodrick that Tori had stepped away from the desk so as not to get her friend into trouble.

Down the hallway, she passed by his assistant's closed door. She wouldn't be in today because it was the weekend.

Diana knocked on the door to his office.

"Come in."

When she entered, Rodrick sat behind his desk, and his eyes widened in surprise.

"What are you doing here?" he asked.

"I want you to hear me out."

"Wait, before you get started—"

"No, Rodrick, enough." She slammed her purse onto a guest chair and leaned across the desk on her hands. "I've had enough of your threats. Enough of your ultimatums. You want a fight, then you'll get a fight on your hands."

Her insides shook, but she was angry, too. After eight years of misery, Rodrick had turned her into a cowardly creature filled with shame, controlling her with his threats and insults. She continued to allow him to do that. Thanks to Xavier, she embraced her sexuality and no longer felt dirty or embarrassed to share her fantasies. And she would no longer allow Rodrick to cow her.

She waited for the explosion, but nothing happened. Instead, Rodrick stood up and said, quite nicely, "I don't want to fight with you, Diana."

She gawked at him. "What?"

She expected to be cursed, yelled at, called names, and possibly even thrown out. She did not expect for Rodrick to be so calm and...*nice.*

"Have a seat. Please."

She studied his face. Where was the outrage and vitriol she'd become so used to?

"Please, Diana." He gestured toward the chair in front of him.

Slowly, she perched her bottom on the edge of the seat, clutching her purse on her knees.

"I've been doing a lot of thinking, and I owe you an apology."

Diana blinked. Had she entered an alternate universe?

"You're the mother of my child, and my behavior toward you has been completely unacceptable. There's no excuse, really, for how I've treated you. I'm sincerely sorry."

"Come again?"

"From now on, you'll see a change in me. We have a son to co-parent, and we may not be together, but that doesn't mean we can't raise a healthy, well-adjusted kid."

Diana's mouth fell open. "I-I don't know what to say."

"There's nothing for you to say. I'll simply show you I'm a changed man."

"Oh...kay," she said slowly.

"I have something for you. I planned to call you this morning, but since you're here..." He lifted a document from the side of the desk and placed it in front of her.

Diana examined the notarized sheet and gasped. Her eyes flicked up to his. "Is this—did you sign over the deed to the house?"

Rodrick nodded. "I did. You only have to record it at the courthouse, and it's official. You never have to worry about where you're going to live. You can sleep easy at night knowing that you, Dre, and Camille will always have a place to stay."

"Rod, I don't know what to say. Why did you do this?"

"Like I said, I've been thinking, and this was the right thing to do."

Pressing a hand to her chest, Diana said, "I'm overwhelmed. I didn't expect any of this when I walked in."

"I know."

She glanced at the deed transfer and eyed him warily. "This is legitimate?"

"You used to work with me. You know it's legit."

"Thank you, Rod. I, um...obviously, I'm surprised."

"You expected a fight."

"Yes, I did." She cleared her throat. "Does this mean you're not going to try to get full custody of Dre?" she asked.

"Our current custody arrangement will remain intact. You're a good woman, Diana. I'm lucky my son has you as a mother."

He sounded so sincere, she almost believed him.

Diana snatched up the deed before he changed his mind. "Okay, then. I guess we'll talk soon." She rose from the chair but lingered, staring at him.

"Sounds good." Rodrick smiled at her. *Smiled.*

She couldn't recall the last time she saw him direct that expression in her direction.

After one last glance of disbelief, Diana left his office.

****

Diana arrived at Xavier's house later that night, after dinner with her son and a long conversation with Camille. Her cousin had finally landed a job working in the bursar's office at the University of Washington. She started in two weeks and Diana couldn't be happier she'd found a position on her own.

The more she thought about the encounter with her ex, it didn't make sense that Rodrick had done such a complete one-eighty. After some consideration, she came to the conclusion that more than simply thinking about their situation had prompted the drastic change.

She rang the bell and waved at the camera on the outer wall. Thomas opened the door.

"Hi. Is Xavier in?"

"Yes, Miss Cambridge. Come right in."

Xavier explained Thomas would always address her in a more formal manner, and she'd given up encouraging him to simply call her Diana. He led her into the great room.

"I'll let Mr. Johnson know you're here."

"Thank you."

Not much time had passed, but she already felt like a stranger in this house. She looked out the window to the outdoor patio and pool, where she and Xavier had enjoyed several lazy days playing in the water.

His reflection appeared in the window and her heart squeezed tight. Turning to face him, she fought the urge to rush into his arms. He looked so good and yummy in white linen pants, his dark hair swept away from his face and hanging loose down his back.

She rubbed her hands together. "Hi."

"Hi."

"I saw Rodrick today."

"How did that go?"

"Exceptionally well. Better than expected."

"Oh?"

"He signed over the deed to the house and promised not to try to take Dre. He even apologized for his behavior over the years."

"Sounds like you had a good meeting."

"Is that all you have to say?" Diana asked.

"Should I say something else?"

"I know what you did. You talked to him, didn't you?"

"I plead the fifth."

"After I told you not to."

He tilted his head, his eyes warm but focused. "Did you really think I would let him get away with hurting you?"

"What if your actions backfired?"

"Backfiring was not an option. I was protecting you and Andre."

"Even after everything I said? You still did that for us?"

"When I told you I loved you and your son, I meant it. You're special to me, and even if you were angry with me for meddling, it would have been worth it to put your mind at ease. You deserved that. You didn't deserve what he was doing to you."

Diana moved closer, coming within touching distance of him. "So I guess it's true what they say about you Johnsons, huh? You do whatever you want?"

The right corner of his mouth lifted. "We get whatever we want, too."

"And what do you want?" she asked, fishing for a compliment.

"You. Andre. In my life."

"That would mean our indefinite separation should come to an end."

He placed his hand on her waist and tugged her closer. "Then so be it," he said.

Diana cupped his jaw. "Thank you," she whispered.

"No need to thank me. I made you a promise, and I intended to keep it. I won't allow anyone to hurt you." A fierce light came into his dark eyes. "I wasn't going to push, but I wasn't giving up, either." His hand lifted against the back of her head, and he drew her mouth closer to his. "You're mine now, Diana Cambridge. And I don't let go without a fight." He kissed her and she melted against him, lifting her arms around his neck and pressing against his hard body.

"Mmm." She traced the tip of her tongue along his lip, content that she was back in his arms, where she needed to be. "Tell me something."

"Mhmm." He kissed her neck, sending tingles of desire down her spine. She tilted her head to the side so he could suck her neck.

"How in the world did you get Rodrick to do such a one-eighty? You didn't do anything crazy, did you?"

Soft puffs of air hit her neck when he laughed. "Me? When have I ever done anything crazy?"

CHAPTER TWENTY-NINE

Diana slowly hung up her mobile phone.

"Who was that?" Camille asked.

She and Diana sat in the kitchen eating the last of a carton of salted caramel ice cream.

"Rodrick." Diana sat in stunned silence for a minute. "He called to make sure I recorded the deed and wanted to know if I needed anything else." So much had changed in a week.

"That was nice of him," Camille said.

"I know. I guess he's serious about changing."

"That man-to-man talk worked really well." Camille dipped into her bowl.

"It sure did."

They looked at each other and burst out laughing.

Andre came racing into the room. "Mommy, let's go!"

Diana sighed. Her son had been antsy all day, ever since she mentioned they'd be going to Xavier's for dinner. "You're more excited than I am."

"Cause I'm hungry, and Thomas makes good baked chicken."

Diana and Camille laughed.

"Yes, he does. Still, you act like you haven't eaten all day. Thomas is going to think I starve you." She scraped the remnants of ice cream from the bottom of the bowl. "All right, let's get out of here. See you later, Camille."

"Bye." Her cousin gave her a flutter wave.

In the driveway, Diana pulled up short. Xavier's driver, Cliff, was standing in front of the blue SUV.

"Hello Andre, Miss Cambridge. Mr. Johnson sent me to pick up you and Andre. He also asked me to give you this." He held out a sealed envelope.

Diana took it. "What is this?"

Cliff shrugged, glanced at her son, and then proceeded to stand beside the SUV with a small camera trained on her.

Diana's heart started racing, and beside her, Andre had his mouth covered, his eyes bright and excited. "Open it, Mommy."

"Do you know what this is?" Diana asked.

"I promised not to tell."

Carefully, she tore open the envelope and read the contents aloud.

Dear Diana,

You and Andre have brought happiness and excitement into my life. I hope you'll embrace the fun I have planned for you this evening and participate in a scavenger hunt. Upon completion, a very important question will be waiting for you. Make sure you read each clue out loud. Cliff will be filming.

Let the games begin.

Xavier

Clue: Where can you find the best, bad-for-you burgers in Seattle?

"Burger Escape." Diana bit her bottom lip and looked around the neighborhood, wondering if Xavier was nearby, watching.

"Let's go, Mommy!" Andre tugged on her hand.

Diana laughed. "Okay, okay."

Cliff opened the back door, and Diana settled in with her son beside her in the booster seat Xavier had obviously had installed for this occasion.

They rode down to the pier and found Jaclyn waiting in front of the bench where she and Xavier had eaten—which now seemed so long ago.

"Jaclyn!"

"Congratulations!"

They hugged, and Diana fought back tears as she took the next envelope her friend handed over.

Diana, I've eaten here a few times since we did together, but it's not as satisfying as when we ate and talked that night. You opened my eyes that night, and I started to realize that what was missing from my life could have been right in front of me all along.

Xavier

Clue: Have some cheesecake, on me.

"Where to, ma'am?" Cliff asked.

Diana laughed, covering her face. "I guess we're going to Nan's Cheesecake Shop."

"Bye!" She and Jaclyn hugged again and then she hurried into the SUV.

On the ride to the store, Diana asked her son, "Did you know about all this?"

He nodded vigorously. "I helped." His face was bright and excited. No wonder he'd been in such a hurry to leave the house.

Diana kissed his cheek. "Thank you, baby."

The aromatic fragrance of freshly ground coffee and the sweet scent of freshly baked desserts greeted Diana when she entered Nan's. Diners openly ogled her, Andre, and her one-man camera crew as they strolled to the back of the shop.

Diana walked up to the long chrome counter, underneath which a glass case displayed the week's choice of cheesecakes on white pedestal cake stands. She waved at Nan, the owner, grinding coffee beans in the back.

"Hello, love." Nan, an older British woman with white hair and a buxom build, shuffled over. "I have something for you." She came back with a box of cheesecake and an envelope on top.

Diana,

Nan and I are good friends now since I come by her shop way more than I should, thanks to you.

Xavier

Diana giggled. "I told you it was good cheesecake," she murmured to herself, and continued reading.

Clue: You'll find the next clue at your favorite clothing store.

"Thank you for the cheesecake," she said, taking the box.

"Here's one for your little man," Nan said, handing her another box.

"Thank you!" Andre said.

"You're lucky. You get dessert before dinner," Diana said. They left the shop and ate their desserts on the way to Torrid Ashley.

Inside, Camille was waiting.

"You knew about this?" Diana asked in shock.

"Yes, and I was dying to tell you, believe me. I'm so excited!" Camille pulled her into an exuberant hug. "You have no idea how hard it was to keep this a secret." She took Diana's hand. "Come on, Joan and I picked out a couple of dresses for you."

They scurried to where a saleswoman with burgundy hair and frameless glasses waited holding two dress options—an azure blue maxi dress with batwing sleeves and a red sleeveless dress with an empire waist. After trying on both outfits, Diana settled on the blue dress with a pair of kitten heels. Complete with a chunky necklace, earrings, and a matching bracelet, Diana surveyed her reflection in the mirror outside the fitting room.

"You look gorgeous, Mommy," Andre said.

"You think so?" Diana did a three-sixty turn in the mirror.

"Yes!" Andre said enthusiastically.

"Definitely," Camille added.

Joan came over and handed Diana another envelope. "Your next clue," she said.

Diana tore it open.

Diana,

You're almost done.

Clue: I'm inviting you to your favorite place, where you feel most at peace.

Xavier

Tears filled Diana's eyes, and she brushed away the single one that slipped from her eye.

"Don't cry, Mommy. It's a good surprise. I promise."

"I know, sweetie. These are happy tears, believe me." She took her son's hand. "Thank you," she said to the saleslady. She pulled Camille into a hug. "Thank you."

"Congratulations," Camille whispered. "I'm glad I was able to be a part of it."

They left with lots of waving and loud good-byes from Camille and Joan. The ride to Xavier's home was made in silence. Diana's heart beat even faster with excitement and nervousness. They climbed the slope to his hilltop abode, and Cliff parked in the driveway. The sounds of the night surrounded her and Andre as they walked hand in hand to the front door.

As she approached, it was opened from the inside. Expecting Xavier, her heart leaped into her throat, but Thomas stood waiting for them.

"Good evening, Miss Cambridge. Andre." He stepped aside so they could enter, and Cliff handed off the camera to him. "Mr. Johnson isn't here right now, but he asked me to give you this." Thomas handed her an envelope.

Diana,

There's a change of clothes for Andre in the spare bedroom. Once he's dressed, follow his instructions. He's in charge.

See you soon.

Xavier

"I'm in charge," Andre said.

"You are way too excited about that part," Diana said with a laugh. "All right, mister. Let's get you changed."

In the spare bedroom, a miniature tuxedo lay across the bed. Diana helped Andre get changed and choked up at the result. "You look so handsome and dapper." She smoothed the tie over his chest.

"Thank you." Andre blushed.

They exited the bedroom, and Thomas continued filming. Andre seemed to know where he was headed, leading the way into the kitchen. There was still no sign of Xavier, though.

"Remember the note said you have to follow my instructions?" her son asked.

"Yes," Diana said slowly.

Andre went over to the kitchen table and picked up a satin blindfold laying across it.

"Wait a minute, what's going on?" Diana said. She glanced at Thomas, who held the camera to his eye.

"Xavier said you have to do what I say," Andre reminded her.

"But a blindfold?"

"Trust me, Mommy. I'll walk you outside."

"You won't let me fall?"

He shook his head. "I won't. I promise."

Diana secured the satin over her eyes and Andre took her hand.

"I'll walk slowly," Andre said.

And he did, taking careful steps as he led her out the back door of the kitchen onto the cobblestone path at the back of the house. She knew exactly where she was and where she was being led to. The koi pond.

Andre came to stop. "Okay, you can take off the blindfold now."

Diana did as her son said and he took the blindfold from her. She blinked rapidly to adjust her eyes. What she saw made her gasp.

Most of the lights on the property had been turned off, and a row of lanterns lined either side of the pathway to the pond. At the end, in lights, were the words, *Will you marry me?*

As tears rushed to her eyes, Diana covered her trembling lips with both hands. She was overwhelmed. Elated.

She looked left to right. Where was he?

All of a sudden, Xavier stepped out of the darkness. Dressed in a tuxedo like her son, he walked slowly toward her. A big, domineering force, his dreadlocks loose and cascading down his shoulders and back.

He stopped a few feet away and lowered to one knee. Opening a small black box, he revealed a pear-shaped diamond. Diana could barely see Xavier through the tears, but his expression was earnest and loving.

"I knew the kind of woman I wanted for a wife, but I never knew if I'd ever find her. Then I did. That woman is you. I can't imagine growing old with anyone else. I want to be a family with you and Andre, and I want to grow our family with more children. I will provide for you and protect you to my very last breath. Andre has already given his blessing, so now I need to know—Diana, would you do me the honor of becoming my wife?"

She sniffed. "There's only one answer for me to give, Xavier. That answer is yes."

"Yay!" Andre jumped up and down.

Xavier slid the ring on her finger and then stood. He pulled Diana into his arms and placed a gentle, almost chaste kiss on her mouth.

"I love you so much," she whispered. Later, when they were alone, she'd properly thank him for the wonderful surprise.

Xavier grinned at her and then lifted Andre into his arms. "You did an excellent job."

Andre nodded vigorously. "I think so, too," he said.

They laughed and then huddled into a three-person hug.

EPILOGUE

"I'm shocked," Corinne said. "I know everything that happens in this company but didn't have a clue about you and Xavier Johnson."

It was the end of the day on Friday in the atrium of the Johnson Enterprises building. Employees milled around the group of four comprised of Naylene, Corinne, Jaclyn, and Diana. A week had passed since the engagement, but this was the first time Diana had met with the other two women in their circle of friends.

Corinne looked up from the pear-shaped rock glinting on Diana's extended hand. Her gaze shifted to Jaclyn. "And you knew about this?"

"I had an inkling," she said, slanting a glance at Diana, who blushed. "I was excited to participate in the proposal. Diana and Xavier make the perfect couple. I don't know why I didn't see it before."

"You were too busy trying to set her up with Bryant, that's why," Corinne said drily.

"True." Jaclyn laughed.

"So what does this mean?" Naylene asked, looking discomfited. "You won't sit at lunch with us anymore?"

"Of course, I will! We'll still be friends," Diana assured her.

Corinne crossed her arms. "I guess I have to keep my comments about your fiancé to myself from now on," she grumbled.

Diana placed a hand on her hip. "You can talk about him, but know that he's all mine."

"I hate you and I'm jealous, but congratulations." Corinne pulled her into a warm hug. "Are you keeping your executive assistant job for Trenton, or are you going to start working up close and personal for Mr. Dreadlocks?"

"I don't think Trenton would forgive Xavier for taking me away. I'm keeping my job. At least for now." Conversations with Xavier made her consider taking a position with the Johnson Foundation. She saw an opportunity to use her administrative skills in a different way, and was particularly interested in the children programs.

"And I'd like to keep my job, thank you very much," Jaclyn added.

The elevator doors opened and Xavier strode out amongst a group of employees. His long hair was pulled back into a low ponytail, and he looked regal and majestic in a royal blue Ozwald Boateng suit with a tribal print tie.

When he saw her, his dark brown eyes lit up with affection. She'd grown accustomed to that expression in his eyes. It stirred a multitude of emotions to know she was unconditionally valued and respected, and that all facets of her character were loved and appreciated in equal measure.

"Hello, ladies," he said, his deep voice vibrating over her skin.

She wondered how long those sensations would continue, but suspected this man would always make her feel warm and tingly all over.

"Hello," her three friends sang in unison.

He chuckled and took her hand. "Ready to go?"

Diana nodded. "See you all later," she said to her friends, waving.

"Bye," they called in the same singsong voice, waving.

Cliff waited outside the building beside the SUV and nodded respectfully in greeting when they approached. Diana climbed in first, and when they were settled in the car, he asked, "Where to? Going home?"

"No." Xavier extended an arm across the back of the seat. "I have a taste for something different. I think I want..." He let his voice fall away in mock deep thought. "I want fried ravioli and gooey butter cake. Take us to the airport."

Diana slid across the seat. "We're going to Missouri?" she asked, excited.

He nodded his head, eyelids lowered halfway over his eyes. "Presidential suite," he murmured, his voice husky.

Andre was with his father this weekend, so they had the next couple of days to themselves. The thought of reconnecting in the same place where they'd first made love made Diana's heart beat faster.

"I don't have anything to wear, sir," she purred, gazing up at him.

"You can buy what you need when we get there." He lowered his voice and placed his lips near her ear. "Trust me, you won't be needing much."

Giggling, Diana placed a hand to his chest. "You are so bad." She rested her head in the crook of his shoulder.

Xavier squeezed his arm around her. "You've got me all wrong. I'm the good one, remember?"

Diana lifted her gaze to him again. "You are. And I'm glad you're all mine."

His lips pressed a soft, affectionate kiss to her hairline, and Diana settled against his chest.

Neither Xavier nor Rodrick had told her what they discussed the day Xavier talked to her ex-husband, and she realized she didn't need to know.

Xavier encapsulated all the qualities she'd been looking for in a mate. As a protector and provider, he embodied qualities she hadn't even considered. He loved and appreciated all facets of her personality, and she loved and appreciated all facets of his.

They were compatible in every way, and she knew without a doubt, that this was her one true love—the man she was meant to spend the rest of her life with.

Bonus Content

Ivy and Lucas

Tonight was her wedding night.

Ivy was nervous, but not the bad kind of nervous. The happy kind of nervous. She was finally marrying the man of her dreams, the man she should have married years ago, the man she'd loved since her early twenties, and the father of her daughter.

Her family and bridesmaids had congregated in one of the bedrooms of her mother's house. The nine bridesmaids consisted of her maid of honor Cynthia, her executive assistant and friend of many years, Atlanta cousins Simone and Ella, three sorority sisters, two friends she'd known since prep school, and her sister-in-law, Alannah.

Each bridesmaid wore a gold sequined dress of varying designs and a slit up the left thigh. All the bridesmaids would carry an all-white bouquet of peonies, bougainvillea, and roses down the aisle. With her wedding dress she'd gone the nontraditional route, and her Aunt Sylvie designed a one-of-a-kind halter in a champagne color. The simple A-line gown gave her an elegant silhouette and contained no embellishments except for her and Lucas's initials embroidered together in the train.

Ivy sat very still before a gilded mirror as the makeup artist put the finishing touches on her face, and her mother and Aunt Sylvie looked on.

When a knock sounded at the door, the women in the room halted their chatter.

"I'll get it," Alannah said. She hurried to the door.

Through the mirror's reflection, Ivy saw Lucas's best man, Roarke Hawthorne standing in the hallway in a black tuxedo. He'd flown in from Atlanta on his brother's private jet with four of the nine members of Lucas's wedding party.

A smile creased his handsome face. "Good evening, ladies. Lucas asked me to give a message to Ivy. He needs to talk to her."

An uncomfortable silence filled the room, and Alannah's worried gaze met Ivy's in the mirror.

"He can't see her before the wedding," Constance said.

"He doesn't want to see her," Roarke explained. "He only wants to talk to her. He's down the hall and standing around the corner. He needs to speak to her for a few minutes, that's all." He looked at Ivy.

Nervously, Ivy licked her lips. Was something wrong? Had Lucas changed his mind?

Lucas hadn't given any indication that he didn't want to get married. He seemed quite happy leading up to the wedding. They already lived as a family with their daughter, and the ceremony was simply a formality, delayed because she wanted to be sure he had his family present, and that had been accomplished.

"I don't like this," Sylvie murmured.

Everyone else was quiet in the room.

Ivy rose slowly from the chair and walked to Roarke. At the door, she turned back to the group. "I'll be right back. I'm sure everything's fine," she said, reassuringly.

She gathered her skirt and followed behind Roarke, who guided her to the end of the hallway. "She's here," he announced.

"Hey, princess." The minute she heard Lucas's calm, reassuring voice, she knew the bundle of nerves in her stomach had no business being there. Roarke left to give them privacy, and Lucas's hand came around the corner. "Take my hand, Ivy," he said quietly.

Her dress rustled over the wood floor as she moved closer and took his hand. It swallowed hers, enveloping it in warmth.

"What's going on?" she asked.

"With my traveling and the craziness of the wedding the past few months, we haven't had a chance to talk about what's going to happen tonight. Not in depth, the way I'd like." His deep voice took on a grave quality. "Before we go downstairs and become man and wife, I wanted to tell you how much I appreciate everything you've done for me." His thumb rubbed back and forth across her knuckles. "You've changed my life, and I appreciate our daughter and the decision you made years ago to have her even when I made it clear I didn't want to be a father. I appreciate you giving me another chance to make you happy, and for helping me find my mother and father—my identity—after so many years. I can't even express to you how much I appreciate you giving me that piece of my life. My...past. My birthdate." His voice thickened. "For confirming the memory I had of a woman singing to me was not a false memory. It was real. I wasn't crazy."

Ivy's hands tightened around his.

"I appreciate you, princess. I love you. So much." His voice shook with emotion.

Tears welled in Ivy's eyes. "You can't make me cry," she whispered. "I flew in a makeup artist from LA. I look flawless." She laughed shakily and brushed away a tear that hung on the bottom lashes.

"I definitely do not want to make you cry."

Male laughter sounded from downstairs. Probably the groomsmen.

"I love you, too. I'm so happy I get to become your wife. Finally."

"It's only taken...what? Thirteen years or so?" Lucas asked.

"Something like that." Ivy laughed.

They stood quietly holding hands.

"I can't wait to make you my wife. Finally."

She sensed his happiness and could almost see the way his eyes crinkled and his full mouth curved up at the corners.

"I'm ready."

"Let's say a prayer first. Just the two of us."

Ivy bowed her head and listened to Lucas whisper words of thanks for all their family and friends who would assemble tonight. He asked for grace and blessings on their wedding day and throughout their entire union, for them both, for their daughter, and for their future children. At the end of the short speech, he lifted her fingers to his lips and kissed each one in turn.

Then he let out a deep breath. "Let's do this."

Quietly, they went their separate ways. The next time she saw him, he was waiting for her at the end of the aisle.

****

Lucas looked out over the sea of faces at the open-air ceremony on Constance Johnson's property. Standing with him were his best man Roarke and friends Derrick, Matthew, Antonio, and Xander, two of his foster brothers, and two other friends.

Lanterns and candles covered the property, transforming it into a romantic, dramatic landscape. Glass orbs containing battery-operated tea light candles hung from the trees and adorned the grounds. Lit lanterns lined either side of the aisle leading to the raised platform Constance had erected for the officiant and wedding party to stand on overlooking the lake.

Seated in the front pew were his family. His blood family.

First, the investigator found his mother, Jordana Nobles. At twenty, she'd flown to Panama to live with relatives after leaving him at Grady Hospital in Atlanta. He'd never guessed he'd had Afro-Panamanian roots. Now a teacher, she said leaving him had been the toughest decision she'd ever made. She'd never forgotten him and always regretted she hadn't been stronger and better prepared to take care of her baby boy.

Finding her finally gave Lucas the background he'd needed. He knew his birthday now—September 10th—and he was thirty-nine years old. The memory of a woman with an Afro singing "Rock-a-Bye-Baby" hadn't been false at all. Jordana confirmed she'd sung the song to him numerous times before she left him at the hospital.

After finding his mother, it had been a simple matter to find his father. Rex Stanton was twenty-five at the time of his birth, and married. His wife had never known about Lucas's existence, and having him come into his life created quite an uproar in Rex's multi-decade marriage. But once the smoke settled, he and his father started a tentative relationship.

On his mother's side, Lucas had three sisters, two of whom continued to live in Panama, and one who resided in south Florida. On his father's side, he had three brothers and two sisters.

The two harpists started the wedding march, and Lucas straightened while the guests stood and turned their attention to the back of the aisle. He didn't even realize he was holding his breath until Ivy made an appearance on the arm of her oldest brother, Cyrus. She was radiant, with flowers in her hair and a beautiful dress that showed off the shoulders he loved to kiss each night.

They'd been living together for several years, but this was it, and all he could think about was how much he loved her. That this vision, this very amazing woman, was finally going to become his wife. He could barely fight back the emotion that clogged his throat. Tears filled his eyes, and he pressed his lips together to keep from sobbing.

As she glided closer, he saw she was having difficulty, too. Eyes watery. Lips trembling.

When the officiant asked, "Who gives this woman to be married to this man?" Lucas simply looked at her, letting her know with his eyes how much he adored her.

He saw the exact moment when she calmed. How a silent breath left her parted lips, and the tears cleared from her eyes.

And then she smiled.

****

"Mother, are you okay?"

Ivy found Constance in the sunroom. They'd all been searching for her under the tent for the last twenty minutes, when Ivy thought to come up to the house.

"Yes, my dear, I'm fine, but I feel a little tired and wanted some quiet time to myself. Away from all the revelry."

"Are you sure you're okay?"

"Yes, of course. But you can stay with me if you like."

Leaving the door ajar, Ivy walked farther into the room and sitting beside her mother, took her hand. She seemed lost in her own world.

"Are you thinking about Father?" Ivy asked.

"How can you tell?"

"I thought about him a lot today."

She'd thought about him a lot lately, in general. He'd been opposed to expanding the family's restaurant business through franchising, but that's the direction they'd chosen to go in. They'd kept their high-end restaurant, Ivy's, private, but worked out a franchising arrangement for the casual dining chain, The Brew Pub. They'd seen particularly strong results selling Americana overseas.

As COO of the restaurant group, she spearheaded the expansion. She understood her father's concerns about maintaining quality and worked closely with the consultants to make sure the family's stellar brand reputation would be maintained. Not only for their sakes, but because she wanted to make her father proud.

Snuggling close to her mother, she wrapped her arm around her arm and threaded their fingers together. "I wish he could have met Lucas."

Constance nodded slowly. "He would have liked him, I think."

"I think so, too. After he gave him hell, of course."

"Oh, of course."

They both laughed.

"How are you feeling?" Constance asked.

"Happy. Exuberant. It's the best day of my life."

"Mmm, that's nice. But I mean, how are you feeling physically? No morning sickness?"

Ivy looked into her mother's dark eyes. "What?"

"You heard me."

"Mother, how did you know?"

"I *know*."

"I only confirmed my pregnancy this morning. I haven't even told Lucas yet."

"Well, your secret's safe with me until you're ready to share." Constance patted her hand. "We need to pray for a boy so Katie can have that little brother she so desperately wants."

Ivy laughed. "I think she'll be happier than I am for this pregnancy."

"They're in here," Xavier's voice called from the doorway. The next thing Ivy knew, the entire family was traipsing into the sunroom.

Katie skipped over and sat on the other side of her grandmother. "Grandma, we were worried," she said.

"I didn't mean to worry you, my love. Grandma is fine. Just tired."

"Are you sure that's all it is?" Cyrus asked, his frowning face and heavy bass voice filled with concern.

"I promise you I'm fine. Now you all sit and stop hovering or I'll have to kick you out."

Trenton sat in an armchair and pulled Alannah onto his lap. Terri, pregnant again with baby number four, collapsed onto the loveseat beside her husband, Gavin. Lucas and Xavier stood behind the chair his fiancée Diana was seated in. Cyrus went to stand in front of the window while his wife, Daniella sank into the space next to Ivy.

As always happened when the family was together, they started talking and laughing, teasing and joking.

Daniella shared real-time video of Lily, her newborn, sleeping in the crib.

"I thought it would get easier, but I'm as protective of her as I am of Michael. Cyrus carried Michael everywhere and barely let his feet touch the floor. He's doing the same thing to Lily."

"And you're just as bad," Cyrus said from across the room.

"I admit it. I'm terrible." Daniella pursed her lips.

"It will get easier," Constance assured her daughter-in-law.

"Just think," Trenton said, "by the time Gavin and Terri, for example, have the last one, the kid will be running around with scissors and playing with matches in a pile of dry leaves."

A round of laughter went up in the room, and Gavin tossed a cushion at his brother, hitting Alannah in the head.

"Hey!" Trenton and Alannah exclaimed, and Alannah rubbed her temple.

"You're married to him now, so all his lumps are your lumps, too," Gavin said.

The quiet chirping of an electronic device brought the conversation and laughter to a halt. Cyrus pulled out a phone from his breast pocket, and one eyebrow lifted.

He looked at the group. "This news came earlier than expected. Since we're all here together, I might as well tell you what's going on. According to the unofficial word from my contact at the Brewers Association, we did it. Last quarter's statistics are in, and we beat Anheuser-Busch. We are now the number one beer company in the nation."

Ivy's mouth fell open as gasps filled the room.

Then everyone erupted into cheers. There were hugs all around as the family celebrated a seemingly unsurmountable goal they'd tried to achieve for years.

Cyrus looked at his mother, and her eyes softened on him.

"We have to toast this accomplishment," Gavin said.

While they talked excitedly about the business milestone, Gavin rushed out of the room. He came back with two servers who proceeded to pour champagne and carbonated apple juice into glass flutes. Ivy took one of the non-alcoholic drinks, hoping no one noticed.

"What are we toasting to?" Trenton asked when the servers had left.

"Good fortune and hard work?" Gavin suggested.

"Mother?" That came from Xavier.

All eyes turned to Constance. "Oh my," she said, a hand pressed to her chest.

The room fell silent as they awaited her words.

Constance looked around the room, a wistful smile on her face. "Well...you did it. All of your hard work paid off. I couldn't be any prouder than I am in this moment. What you've accomplished is unprecedented. But even more important than the status or the money is how you did it." Her eyes swept the room filled with family members avidly listening to the words coming from her mouth. "You did it together. As a family." Her eyes glimmered with tears, and Ivy looped an arm across her shoulders. "My wonderful, adoring family, that's growing by leaps and bounds it seems. Another baby on the way." She smiled at Terri, who sniffed and swiped away a tear. "My new son-in-law and future daughter-in-law." Her gaze encompassed Lucas and Diana to the right. "Trenton and Alannah, who now that they're settled into their new home will hopefully make me a grandmother again very soon." Soft laughter filled the room. "You all have done an amazing job. You've built on our legacy for the next generation." She touched Katie's chin. "I'm so proud of you. Each and every one of you. Your father is watching, and he's proud, too. And bragging quite obnoxiously, I'm sure."

More soft laughter.

Constance stared at the clear wine in her glass, and tears glimmered in her eyes. It hurt. It hurt like hell to see the pain her mother suffered through, even in the midst of her happiness.

Constance swallowed and lifted her gaze. "Congratulations, my dear, dear children. Congratulations on a job well done." She lifted her glass.

"Here! Here!"

The room filled with the tinkling sound of the flutes touching together, and then everyone took a sip from their glass.

Ivy looked across the room at her new husband and found his gaze already on her. She couldn't wait to tell him the good news—that they'd be expanding their family sooner rather than later. That he would experience the journey of bringing life into the world, from the very beginning this time. The cherry on top of tonight's delicious dessert of a beautiful wedding and accomplishing a lifelong goal in business.

I love you, she mouthed.

The smile he sent her way made her heart constrict in happiness. *I love you, too,* he mouthed back.

MORE STORIES BY DELANEY DIAMOND

Love Unexpected series
The Blind Date
The Wrong Man
An Unexpected Attraction
The Right Time
One of the Guys
That Time in Venice (coming soon)

Johnson Family series
Unforgettable
Perfect
Just Friends
The Rules
Good Behavior

Latin Men series
The Arrangement
Fight for Love
Private Acts
The Ultimate Merger
Second Chances
More Than a Mistress (coming soon)
Hot Latin Men: Vol. I (print anthology)
Hot Latin Men: Vol. II (print anthology)

Hawthorne Family series
The Temptation of a Good Man
A Hard Man to Love
Here Comes Trouble
For Better or Worse
Hawthorne Family Series: Vol. I (print anthology)
Hawthorne Family Series: Vol. II (print anthology)

Bailar series (sweet/clean romance)
Worth Waiting For

Stand Alones
Passion Rekindled
A Passionate Love
Still in Love
Subordinate Position
Heartbreak in Rio (part of Endless Summer Nights)

Free Stories
www.delaneydiamond.com

ABOUT THE AUTHOR

Delaney Diamond is the USA Today Bestselling Author of sweet, sensual, passionate romance novels. Originally from the U.S. Virgin Islands, she now lives in Atlanta, Georgia. She reads romance novels, mysteries, thrillers, and a fair amount of nonfiction. When she's not busy reading or writing, she's in the kitchen trying out new recipes, dining at one of her favorite restaurants, or traveling to an interesting locale. She speaks fluent conversational French and can get by in Spanish.

Enjoy free reads and the first chapter of all her novels on her website. Join her mailing list to get sneak peeks, notices of sale prices, and find out about new releases.

www.delaneydiamond.com

CPSIA information can be obtained
at www.ICGtesting.com
Printed in the USA
LVOW08s1020300417
532745LV00002B/360/P